DEEP TISSUE

CONFESSIONS OF A MASSAGE THERAPIST

SIMMS BOOKS PUBLISHING

DEEP TISSUE

CONFESSIONS OF A MASSAGE THERAPIST

Simms Books Publishing

SIMMS BOOKS PUBLISHING

Publishers Since 2012

Published By Simms Books Publishing

Jonesboro, GA

Copyright © James R Simms, 2016

All rights reserved. No part of this book may be reproduced, scanned, or distributed in any print or electronic form without permission. Please do not participate in or encourage piracy of copyrighted materials in violation of the author's rights. Purchase only authorized editions.

Library of Congress Cataloging in Publication Data

James R Simms

Deep Tissue Confessions of a Massage Therapist

ISBN: 978-0-9983311-0-2

Printed in the United States of America

Book Arrangement by Simms Books Publishing

Cover by Urias Brown, Michael Shield

Studios-urias@michaelshieldstudio.com

Dedicated to all Massage Therapists who are in the struggle to keep the culture, purpose and goals of what you do professional, abiding by a creed and standard, to Manipulate Soft Tissue. To All Therapists who have tried to work within those guidelines as much as they could, this is part of your story. Some of us have tried and failed to live up to that creed; breaking the code of ethics. Could it have been a matter of money and/or pleasure? Your guess is as good as mine. Here is a story we all know a lot about first hand.

"Rolling, gliding, pushing, pulling, tugging, these hands are at war. Stroking, pinching, grasping, cupping, and caressing...again these hands are at war! Delivering pleasure where there once lay pain, techniques unmatched! Can I please say it again!? These hands are at war, fighting a formidable adversary but the plan is to give in...Yes, you heard me right. Giving in to all the wants and needs of the flesh and still victorious in defeat, for it is not a loss; these hands are at war, I tell you yet again. Peacemakers, stress relievers at best... at war!! War with the flesh..."

Confessions- statements made by a person or group that may shed some light on a subject that may or may not have been front page news. Yeah you guessed it right! Some secrets are being revealed. 'The Art of Massage' and its therapeutic wonders have been around for well over 4,000 years, practically since the beginning of time, and none of these stories and personal experiences are to be connected in any way to its rich long history. None the less, as long as massage has been around I'm sure its presence has not been without sexual innuendo and connotations due to its levels of intimacy. If you poled 100 people on giving the first words or phrase that comes to mind when you hear "Massage Therapist," I have no doubt that some word referring to sex or the act of sex would be in the top 5. Sad but true, this idiosyncrasy was not created by itself, it had help.

Swedish

"Popping that cherry! I can smell you, your newness leaks from every opening of your body...you shake as my hands touch you and you jump at the grasp of my hands on your back. Calm down, you're in good hands."

I hadn't fully set my table up before she was all over me, pulling
t my scrubs; she wildly grabbed the head of my penis and tugged right
hrough my pants. I wrestled with her for a minute then gave in, I hadn't
lanned on having sex with her but she was persistent.

"Come on! Give it to me!" she yelled as she fought to remove my
enis out of my scrubs.

trawberry lip gloss, mint chocolate, garlic, tomato sauce, our tongues
ntertwined as our bodies crashed into one another, manicured fingers
lowed through strands of hair, accent scents of linen and opium oils fill
he air. I moaned as she rocked her hips back and forth, my arms
tretched out as my hands rubbed and caressed her. With every rock our
odies met, swaying motion of her hips ignited the center of her love
nto my abdomen and it welcomed a thrust as I entered her deeper,
ending waves of pleasure through her inner walls. Peering up, I grasped
 breast, reaching for a waiting nipple to place in my mouth, as I did
ircles around it, taking in her total beauty. Gorgeous eyes, rounded
lmonds, surround jet black precious stones, the envy of the world. Skin
o supple and dark, delightfully delicious, so beautiful I'm aroused by
he sights and sounds; lips are perfect, face of a goddess.

es, only being crafted by a master, and I am engulfed as I basked in her
resence. I'm fully in tune as all of me welcomed all of her. We
limaxed together, over and over again, a kiss and full climatic explosion
etween us, the head of my penis slowly parting her lips, feeling her

wetness as her walls grip it and it goes deeper inside, until she feels every inch sliding past her sweet spot and giving her body a euphoric sensation of millions of waterfalls of pleasure coming down. Her eyes roll to the back of her head. My strokes take her to a place where no one has taken her before, as we both are set ablaze.

Juices flowing from her to me run out and drip down her thighs, then puddling around her buttocks with a line leading to her anus, as the coolness saturates it, making it expand and sending higher vibes of lust as it imitates the feeling of my breath and wet tongue running across it. Our minds race back to when it first happened.

******

Being entered and sucked on, probed lightly, deep long strokes inside her brings back that feeling of being on the edge as she grabbed my back holding on as our bodies danced. The hypnotic rhythm from my hips colliding with her crotch sent waves of heat through my body, as my penis became more erect, pressing against her vaginal walls. She feels the pluses running through my veins as they massage her inner depths. Pleasure and pain a mixture, hitting her spot so it hurts so good. Circling my hips to both grind against her clit and exchange my love outwardly. Our skin to skin contact, my penis stretching and caressing her vagina as tiny explosions go off inside of her, her wetness increases and my libido is energized. Sweat pours out of me and she lies in an ocean of both of our liquids. Grabbing a breast I engulf a nipple with my tongue, playing with it with perfect control of my cyclonic winds, swirl, tease, nibble and suck with the other in care of my other hand, as my fingers twirl and tap her nipple with a wet circular motion. In uneven, stroking, sucking and winding as her body shudders, and my heart skips a beat.

Toes curling, back stiffening, sexual thunder. We both are in a space that's not easy to describe. I can't get enough, it's a trip to paradise looking into her eyes...the softest place on earth...right between her thighs...I'm in heaven...

I've always worked well with my hands, whether it was fixing cars, arts and crafts, fighting or massaging. Now, I wasn't technically trained in doing massages but I just had a pair of great hands that were strong and gifted. I decided to do something with them so I enrolled in massage school the summer after graduating from high school. I really wasn't feeling the whole 2- to 4-year experience on campus; I just wanted to jump right on into the work force. Massage school was 9 months long and was a whole different experience in itself for me. I have to admit, I thought that I was just going to be massaging beautiful women, a class full of women and just me, the only male there to rub all their cares away.

I was wrong; it was not a rub down session or full of beautiful women laying and waiting for me to rub them. So all of my first thoughts of massage school were put to rest on the first day. Once in class, I looked around and the room was made up of young and old, black, white, Asian, Hispanic, male and female, big and small, some beautiful and some not so beautiful. I spent the time picking out who I was going to get to know intimately and who was going to be my massage partner for the remainder of the 9 months.

The instructor stood up and I guess she knew exactly what I had going on in my mind because just then she said,

"Hello, and, ohh fellas, sorry to break it to you but you will not get a choice on who will be your partner or who you will be massaging. Yeah, that's right! Men will be massaging men also."

Ah damn! I did not sign up for this! My plan was foiled by the little hairy lady with the funny accent. I could not believe it and I felt like I had just thrown away good money for this. I was against 'rubbing on some dude;' that was not going to happen. And as I thought to myself, here came the little hairy lady again.

"News flash! To help you guys get more acquainted with each other for the first session, I am doing the pairing for you guys; every year I find that if I allow you to pick, you won't get the full benefit of just why you are here. 'Manipulation of Soft Tissue,' people! That is why you are here! We are not here to rub on people; you can do that at home with your significant other but not in my class room. Do I make myself clear!?"

You could hear a pin drop; everyone must've been thinking the same thing that I was thinking, because the room was silent.

"Again! Do I make myself clear!?"

"Yes!" we all responded in unison.

It was another weird silence that went over the room and I looked around me just to see all the faces in disbelief that they were not there just to 'rub on someone' and it really changed the mood of the room.

"Now that I have your attention," the little hairy lady belted out again,

"Here are the rules of my classroom and you all will follow this to a 'T.' There will be no inappropriate touching, talk or actions at all in this classroom. That will get you thrown out of this program and your money will not be refunded. Lastly, if you call my table a bed, I will cut you!" She continues.

"Massage has been around since man has been around and there are great benefits that come from it...blah blah blah...blah blah blah!

"Who am I fooling? I know that half of you guys in here could care less about the history of massage and its benefits and the other half just want to know how to perform a decent massage to land them a job. Or I could be further away from the truth all together and you all are actually here to learn something and make a difference in the lives of others."

She begins to clap and look around the room, more like a clap of intimidation or plain sarcasm. It's almost like she ran across a group of idiots and she was just rubbing in the intent of just why we were all here and she had to hear it for herself to prove her own thoughts wrong.

"Hey you, yeah you in the back with the green shirt on. Why are you here?"

The middle-aged gentleman was shocked that she would single him out in front of a class of strangers on the first day and have the nerve to ask him why he was here. The look on his face showed that he was not amused at all.

"Well first I am here just like everyone else and that's to learn all there is to know about the Art of Massage."

"Wrong!" she yelled out, cutting him off. You are not here to learn about "The Art of Massage" as she gestured using her hands while emphasizing with quotation marks.

"Nope! No such thing as the Art of Massage, now either you have it or you don't, we just teach you the fundamentals of massage, the history, the techniques, the body, muscles and bones, movement, blah, blah blah...blah blah blah. Now it's on you to take what we teach you and become a Massage Therapist and find a way to incorporate what you learned, along with natural ability to become a great therapist, no "Art" included. You know the old saying, 'You can bring a horse to the water but you can't make him drink,' well, in this case we can teach you all about massage, but it don't translate into "Art" or even you becoming a great Massage Therapist, the rest is on you."

Right then the man asked angrily. "Well what the hell am I here for?"

She responded, "The hell if I know; I just work here!"

"People! People! People! I cannot show you the way or give you the reason that you are here; that very point will have to be determined by you. Whether you pass or not pass, it's up to you and your reason for being here and your passion....it is all on you."

"So basically you not gonna teach us shit?"

The man was on his feet and patting his feet on the floor demanding an answer from the instructor. She looked back in his direction and told him,

"You are free to go if you'd like. I am here to give instruction and that's it; what you get from this class will be what you decided to learn."

"People! I do not teach. I am an instructor and if you cannot follow directions I advise you to leave this program right now. Any takers?"

At that, the man stormed out of the classroom and you could hear him arguing with the lady at the front desk.

"I didn't pay my damn money for this shit, she is rude as hell and I'm not gonna take this shit!"

"Well sir, you will have to go back across the street to take that up with admissions."

The door slammed and there was an awkward silence around the classroom followed by a barrage of conversations going on all at once.

"People! People! People! Ok now that we got that outta the way. Do we now understand that this class is purely instructional? And don't blame me if you don't get it, we have all the resources that you need to become a massage therapist but we can not guarantee that you will be the best that ever did it, or even guarantee you a job after this course is over. It is on you to take what we give you and apply it to the best of your abilities. Any further questions?"

She slumped down into her chair and wiped her forehead while letting a big gust of air out leaning back into her chair.

The class erupted into laughter. I thought to myself, Damn, this lady is crazy but she had a point, you gonna take the time out to spend money on a class, you better have enough passion to see it through and not rely on others to spoon-feed you the info. It is up to you, they give you the tools and instruction and you make it your own. Man didn't know that it would be a lot of politics in a Massage Therapy class, they instruct, we learn. What else would you expect out of it?

The instructor paired us all off and since the old man left, there would be six groups of pairs and the last group would have to be a trio. That worked for me because I was blessed to be part of that trio, two women and one of me, I had no complaints. Right off the bat she gave us definitions of the different types of massage techniques to match up and then after those were done we had to physically demonstrate what stroke belonged to that particular type of massage. It was the basics, nothing too intense, Effleurage, Petrissage and Tapotement.

"People! People! People! You look scared and timid right now. Go ahead and touch them, they not going to bite you! Well unless they are into that type of thing, ahh come on just joking! Now remember another thing, we are not in your bedroom, and for you guys who are hesitant touching another man and this goes for you too ladies; massage is the Manipulation of Soft Tissue, so look at the body as a group of muscles that you are manipulating for one reason only, to move blood and help filter out toxins."

The whole class time she would keep yelling the same thing over and over again like a drill sergeant. I got it and I was in heaven, I couldn't speak for the other guys but then I spoke too soon.

"Excuse me, sir, it looks like you are having too much fun, you have great technique so I'm gonna have you work with those fellas over there." She pointed over to two guys that were partnered up.

I walked over to them and we all gave each other 'the look' like man we really didn't want to be putting our hands on each other.

"Ahh, fellas come on, no biting!" yelling loudly as she hit the ground laughing at us just standing there.

We all just stood around and watched others as they practiced on each other; the ole song and dance 'just manipulating soft tissue' was going to be a very hard tune to dance to.

Massage school was definitely an eye opener for me and I developed a greater appreciation of the history and techniques, not to mention the science of it all. We were not just rubbing on someone and using it as the instructor would say, 'The Prelude to Getting Busy.' Yes, Massage has its own well-known idiosyncrasies; sex and massage go hand in hand. What I learned over that last nine months completely dispelled all of the stereotypes of this practice, and yes, it is definitely a practice. Massage Therapy is the study of the body and we had to learn everything about the body, from biology, anatomy, movement, pathology, epidemiology and all the contraindications, who what when where and how. It was just that deep. It took me every bit of the nine months to look at a human body, male or female, as muscles and know massage was manipulation of soft tissue to derive, at an agreeable state, stability and relaxation.

We had practical instruction along with hands on experience, but one thing that I felt that was not taught was 'situational therapy.' So I would study the best treatments and bring up a condition and list all the possible ways to treat that certain issue. The instructor would ask,

"Can we massage a client with high blood pressure and what type of massage can we do?"

She advised against ever doing a massage on someone with high blood pressure, but she wanted us to think outside the box. I answered back,

"Yes you can because massage can be beneficial to all; it just depends on what type of massage you give them."

"Whoa! Whoa! Whoa! Hold on Mr. Man, you are getting a little too far ahead of the class, so the answer to my original question is yes and no."

I thought outside of the box and figured that there had to be a way to do a massage that wouldn't be contraindicative to someone's issue or condition, and yes I was thinking way outside the box and way past what the instructor was showing us.

"That right there, mister, is what I cannot teach you! Good job! It is on you all too again take what I instruct you on and go above and beyond the theory that is inside these books."

I tried applying that same thought process when we had clinicals, where folks from off the street would come and get a massage. They had specific rules for the public when they came in to get a massage and they had to fill out a sheet beforehand to list any possible issues that they have, but most were never truly honest. I sided on caution when giving a massage, not to fast or hard and really listened to the person's body. I even started off with some questions of my own outside of the intake form, because nine times out of ten, they would lie on the intake form.

I remember I had a lady come in to get a massage and on the intake form it asked if she was on any type of medication or had any alcoholic beverages before she arrived. She was shit faced! She was good with holding her composure while filling out the intake form but when she got on my table it was a different story. As I applied the oil to her back I could smell the alcohol come out of her skin towards the end of the massage she was loopier than two drunk men. When it was time for her to get off the table she was in a deep sleep snoring up a storm, so I allowed her to sleep it off and started massaging her friend and she was just as drunk. Once I was done, the instructor came in and found both ladies on the tables snoring away. They slept for about an hour before they woke up, yelling mad about not getting their massages. That was a classic, two drunk and half naked, belligerent women screaming at the top of their voices.

"I want my money back! I want a massage!"

They got one and it put them to sleep. I dove into the other kinds of massage and did my best to perfect them and it was a gift that paid dividends with the clients that I practiced on. I started to read up on energy, Reiki and Chakra Balancing and applied it every chance that I could. My fellow classmates would always ask,

"What the hell are you doing?" They really had no idea on what the hell I was doing but I was building my repertoire and becoming a better therapist.

I became real good friends with a couple of my classmates and we kinda bounced "situational therapy" topics off of each other which made us better students and massage therapist. I wasn't the only one who had drawn an interest to my philosophy of massage; there were a couple of them, Daniel, Brenda, Chase, and Jessica. We were five the hard way! We were basically teaching each other while the research that each of us took on gained the attention from both classmates and instructors. We each had developed a specialty in massage. I was called 'Dr Feet', that was one of the body parts that most therapists avoided. The majority of them were a bit squeamish when it came to touching another person's feet. I rather enjoyed it. I studied the science of Reflexology and knew that one's stability started and ended at your feet.

There I was, 9 months was over and I was walking across the stage receiving my certificate with plans of getting my state board license and running my own mobile business. I had to just think back on the long days and nights I worked my ass off to get to this point here and I was glad that I got past the part of touching another man. It all had become simple, I am manipulating soft tissue and muscle and that was it, I had given myself that pep talk the whole time that I was faced with massaging another man. I got through it and now I had gained so much more than getting over my fears of touching another man, I had become a certified Massage Therapist who now could see the real value in taking care of my patients and addressing any and all issues pertaining to the body.

Shiatsu

"Getting to the point of this conversation, my hands talk and your body responds."

It had taken me about four months to build up my clientele; I had a good mixture, from dancers, a housewife, a lawyer, a couple who owned a hair salon, a show producer, a chef, and some who would get a massage here and there. Ten years later and my business was still going strong. I was working off word of mouth, that's how I got most of my clients but one client told me that I would get more clients if I advertised in the yellow pages and later I got around to putting a website up. I started with the yellow pages and other social media, and just like I was advised, business picked up. I normally would take clients only four times a week; now I was actually working 6 days out of the week. Thinking back on what I learned in massage school, I was more than equipped to deliver the best massage that my clients would ever receive, and they also came with a whole other bag of issues.

The relationships that I built with most of my clients were borderline friendships. I say borderline because I liked to stay as professional as possible. Our conversations had to do with personal and business, it just seemed that I was also a shrink and massage therapist wrapped up in one. We all have something that we are dealing with, some more than others, and I became their outlet, whether it was problems with their marriages, children, business, social or personal problems, I heard it all. I always had a motto, "never mix business with pleasure," and I stuck to it, but it didn't stop my clients from trying to talk it up. And sex was always the topic. My usual clients would talk about anything under the sun but they had their limits. Going on 10 years plus and the whole landscape of my profession started to change.

One day I was out at the mall advertising my business and I met Shelly. We had exchanged eye contact two times while in the food court and she approached me while I was handing out cards.

"Hello, what are you selling?" she asked.

"Well not really selling anything other than advertising for my mobile massage company."

"Ohh, ok so you are the one giving the massages or is there someone else that does them?"

"No just me would..." she interrupted before I could finish my sentence.

"No thank you. I don't like for strange men to rub on me."

"I understand but I don't 'rub' on anyone."

At that moment all of the instruction I received kicked in and I went into technical mode.

"Actually, I specialize in manipulation of soft tissue and judging by your slight deviation of your left shoulder the purse or briefcase you carry during the week is loaded down with too much stuff; the heels that you're wearing have you hating life by the end of the week; and your lower back has been hurting more days than you can count, keeping you up at night; and the bags you have under your eyes tell the story of long painful nights. How did I do?" She nodded in agreement.

"I can help you with your issues but first you will have to allow me, a strange man, to lay hands on you..."

She chuckled, "Wow, you really sound like you know what you are talking about, and you just read me from head to toe. I really need to stop wearing these heels because my back is all messed up. I will take you up on your offer and get a massage. So where are we gonna do this massage?”

“I can give you a chair massage now so you are comfortable; I also offer table massages where you lay down, semi-clothed or nude.”

“Ohh wow really! I will take the chair massage right now and... Maybe a table massage much much later, don’t need to be showing all my goods to a strange man.”

“Fair enough!” I directed her to the chair and instructed her on how to sit in it and went over the rates, $1 a minute, went over what to expect, and questioned her on how much pressure she would like.

I performed the massage working on stretching her arms, lower and upper back and hips. She got up from the chair.

“Damn! That felt...soo good! I don’t feel the pain anymore; ahh your hands are like silk, I’m gonna have to take you home with me.”

I thanked her and collected my money and handed her a card.

“By the way my name is Shelly,” as she looked over my card, then extended her hand. It was nice to meet you Paul.”

“Likewise,” I responded with a smile as she held onto my hand slowly shaking it.

“I will give you a call and maybe next time it will be for a full body massage.”

I could sense that Shelly was gonna be an issue. She walked away with her heels in hand, head tilted back to the sky mumbling something as she stopped and shook her shoulders, violently bussing out in laughter.

From the time I started my practice, I had women throwing themselves at me left and right; I always stuck to my guns ‘to never mix business with pleasure.' She called me three days later and asked me to meet her where we had first met at the mall. I figured it was harmless, being that she only had a chair massage and nothing else. I entertained her invite and met her again at the food court.

She wanted to talk; we had somewhat started a conversation three days ago on how I got into doing massage and she was also interested in going back to school to pursue doing hair. She had always wanted to own her own salon one day but had become a lawyer instead.

"Sometimes your passion is put to the side for a more practical career." She said, swirling her straw around in her cheese cake concrete sprinkled with honey roasted peanuts.

I'm a single guy, no girlfriend, kids or any attachments, so I was game but still had to honor what I stood on. But this was different; we hadn't actually done a full body massage, which was way more intimate, so we were good. I could see that she was really into me so I had to give her my disclaimer right away.

"Look, I am feeling that you are interested in me, right? Well I don't mix business and pleasure at all and..." she cuts me off.

"No, no I understand fully if we hit it off, but you gave me a massage beforehand and we became intimate it would ruin everything."

Well, damn, she read my mind word for word. I interjected,

"That would be bad for business for sure, you would think that from that point on that I would be having sex with all of my clients, and that's not the case. Furthermore I would have to hang it all up because you wouldn't let me live that down. 'Ohh you have a client? OK so you fucking her like you did me?' "

"Bingo!" She yelled. "Look, I know how it all would end up but I don't want to ruin what you got that's your business and I wouldn't want to come in between that."

We both smiled at each other. That was refreshing that she thought everything through and really made some sense of it, being that from our first encounter she was attracted to me.

"I don't make a habit out of sleeping with my clients and thanks for the insight, I see we think alike."

"Well kind of..," she said nervously. "I don't want a relationship, sex or anything, I just need a good friend and you seem real cool."

We spent the whole day together and the conversation never stopped. We talked about everything, our families, future, things we wanted, and past relationships we made a great connection.

"So how about that massage? Your place or mine?"

I just looked at her, thinking was this going to be a good idea.

"Yours. I have the table with me, it's in my truck."

"Ok then that's that"...as she slurped the remaining ice cream through her straw then dug out the rest of the peanut and cheese cake chunks from her concrete.

"I am in need of a full body massage today! This week has been very stressful. I need something to take my mind off of the worst week in my life!"

Shelly is a defense attorney and she had lost the last two cases this week and both clients were white collar criminals. Both going to jail for embezzlement and with no clear leg to stand on for an appeal, a basic open and shut case. She had worked hours on end to help prove her clients' innocence but with too much evidence against them she couldn't even get a plea deal. Her reputation was set on her being the one to go to... not to go to jail, and this week's cases had tarnished her record. So understandably she was stressed out. She was no short of a genius, finishing law school in three years passing the bar on her first try and actually acing the exam. She buried herself in her work and our meeting in the mall three days ago was somewhat out of the ordinary; she could not be caught dead in the mall. She needed to drown herself into a large cheese cake concrete sprinkled with honey roasted peanuts. She saw me and wondered what all the fuss was about,

I had just finished a massage demo and was explaining the benefits of massage to a large group of pre-med students who had taken a late lunch. While I passed out cards, holding court we caught each other's eyes a couple times. She listened then made her move to introduce herself once the crowd left. She mentioned more than once.

"I'm so happy that I came to the mall that day!"

She had a lot on her mind and I kept that in mind as we drove back to her house, I followed her as she drove like a bat outta hell. I think I must've run four lights, racked up three red light camera tickets and six speeding pictures. She had done really well for herself being so young. Her house was way off the beaten path for real; we passed four large homes which set at the front of the complex and down a long winding road under large pine trees until we reached a clearing where everything seemed to just open up. In the far, was an enormous house which sat behind a circled drive way and rose garden. She hit the garage door opener and two of the three car garage doors opened. We pulled in, parked and exited our cars.

"Nice house."

"Thank you, you can leave your table in your truck. I have one of my own and it's already set up in the sun room. Please go set your oils up and make yourself comfortable, I will be back down in a minute."

"Wait! What? I thought to myself. She had one of her own?"

All the time we spent talking she never told me that she was a massage therapist also. Well damn isn't that something! I thought to myself 'Well maybe not but...why would she have one?'

The sunroom was humongous! Nothing but a wall of windows, no blinds or drapes, and that allowed you to see far off into the distance where a pool, tennis court and gazebo littered the landscape. While I am taking in the atmosphere I do not notice that she had come down and made herself comfortable on the table behind me.

"I'm ready," she whispered in a low smoky voice that made the hairs on the back of my neck stick up, halfway startled and pleasantly surprised as I turned around.

Laying in full view with no clothes on, her head buried deep in the face cradle and feet resting on the bolster pillow. I hadn't really paid that much attention to her body through her pant suit and business tops. Her body was heavenly. Taking in all of her beauty, her jet black spiral curls fall over the left side of the face cradle unrivaled almost touching the floor; her exposed neck line contours gently into her shapely shoulders; following the sun's rays down her dark chocolate skin, my eyes meet at her waist, drawn into a valley that meets the small of her back, ascending to two glorious mounds, firm round and full...I envisioned my hands cupping and grasping each one passionately, separating themselves running my hands down her inner thighs, alternating hand to hand, skin to skin contact, warming the skin as my medium- oil and lust joined in as my hands arms and body engaged in a tussle against her body.

"I'm ready...I'm ready...I'M READY!! I heard her voice jump up and snapped me back out of lala land.

"Huh?! Ohh Ok! I responded gathering myself. The sun...it's real bright in here."

Sure it is..." she said with a smirk as she laid her head back into the face cradle adjusting her hair into a sloppy bun.

"Oh, please concentrate on my lower back legs and feet, they really hurt and need all of your attention."

"Ok no problem." I took a minute to gather myself. Let's face it, there was a heavy attraction there and it was gonna take all of my will power and professionalism to get through this massage without slipping.

Massage is meant to be sensual, intimate, relaxing and beneficial physically; when you add the mental stimulation to the equation it can fulfill all deep desires and fantasies.

Shelly laid there waiting for me to start, taking in deep breaths; I could tell that the anticipation was building. I took a couple deep breaths of my own, not to transfer my nervous energy to her, all the long coaching myself.

"It's just a body, muscles skin and bones, manipulation of soft tissue, disconnect, disconnect, disconnect...Nothing that I haven't done a few hundred times...whew!"

I selected scented oil from my bag, strawberries and dark chocolate, warming the oil in my hands by spreading it both on my hands and forearms. Standing in front of the table I placed my warm hands onto her shoulders. With a slight gasp, she tensed up.

"Relax, relax," I whispered, gliding from her shoulders to the small of her back repeating this motion to warm her back muscles several times.

I could feel that we were in sync, our breathing had calmed and with each and every movement she responded with a moan or twitch. I noticed that her body was very tight and tender to the touch so I incorporated more stretching and light to moderate friction and warming of the muscles, sinking in some pressure here and there to breakup the voids and "crunches" in her skin... a term in therapy that we use when there is a buildup of noticeable stress in the muscles. Most times you will find them in the feet and knots in all other areas of the body.

Shelly was in good shape body tone wise but her muscles were a mess, every inch of her had knots. Our session lasted for about 2 1/2 hours. Once I was done with her massage I didn't wake her up. I let her sleep it off for another half hour. When she woke up she called out to me.

"Hello! Paul! Hello!?"

I had excused myself to the restroom to wash my hands when I heard her calling for me.

"What the hell happened!?" She asked half asleep.

"You fell asleep once I started on your feet and once I finished I wrapped you in the cover and excused myself to the bathroom to wash my hands."

"Ohh wow...how long was I asleep?"

"About 45 minutes I guess and that's normal, plenty of my clients fall asleep when they are getting a massage."

"Well damn you could have been an ax murderer and I could have been killed and wouldn't even know it...damn."

"Take your time getting up," I told her, handing her a bottle of water. "Be sure to always drink plenty of water before and after a massage to help filter the toxins."

"Ahh shit don't give me that technical mumbo jumbo," as she tries to sit up on the table nearly falling off of it.

"Whoa!"

Reaching out to catch her we both fall to the floor. She buries her head into my chest and starts crying. Not a soft little cry either, a balling uncontrollable cry that comes from way deep inside. I tried to console her as much as I could and helped her up off the floor to the couch.

"What's wrong?"

She continued to cry for about another ten minutes and then slowly started to open up about why she was crying.

"I am so sorry, ok. I didn't mean to cry in front of you like this I just had a moment and I lost it, ok. You see...I don't want you to look at me like I'm this crazy woman...but I really do appreciate you not taking advantage of me. I was asleep, I bring you in my home with no one else around and you covered me up and let me sleep. That was so sweet of you."

"Well this is my job, to deliver comfort, relaxation and keep a high level of professionalism at all times, I'm sorry if I offended you in anyway."

"No no no! You were fine you did nothing wrong at all, you actually did everything....right. You don't mind if we can just talk a little more? Do you? Well I know you may have other clients for today but if you don't mind can I pay you for the time and spend the rest of the day with you?"

Damn! I thought to myself. What the fuck did I just get myself into; this is definitely not something that I do Hell! I avoid this type of thing and normally have good radar on "Crazy." Shelly was a very nice young lady, professional, beautiful and seemed to have it all from the outside but was lonely and slowly killing herself at work. I reluctantly said,

"Ok, I can stay; let me call my clients and see about rescheduling for tomorrow."

They did not prepare us for this in massage school at all, the level of intimacy with massage definitely pulled on your human heart strings and

here is a fine line between being professional and crossing the line of no
return, in giving the customer what they want. I had successfully avoided
situations like this over the years, but you always going to have that one.

"Do you know how hard it is to be a young black professional?
The long hours you have to put in, the bar is set so damn high, and
sometimes I get so tired, I just want to quit! I was not always single I had
someone but we didn't last. I guess I put my career before us. I think I
did. I didn't take the time to include a relationship into my life or accept
help to manage my workload, if that makes any sense to you. I wouldn't
necessarily ask anyone to do my work with me but be there supporting
me and telling me when to take a break. You know, giving me balance in
my life, but it's been work work work and I forgot about that part. I even
started to have a messed up value system where my prestige was above
everyone and everything. I worked hard, I am a lawyer, I felt better than
everyone that I felt didn't do a damn thing for me to get this far. I had to
stay up all those nights studying, not them, I did this not them! Then you
made me realize the importance of it all. They were my inspiration and I
didn't see that, I only thought about self. I pushed them all away, I
pushed them away, and the way you looked at me the first time we met
gave me goose bumps. You didn't see the business suit, briefcase, name
tag, the Esquire behind my name, you read me and saw the real me, what
was inside of me, my hurt, my pain, my insecurity, my heart, my mind,
I'm broken and you asked me would I allow you to fix it. The way you
looked at me when I first got on the table undressed and naked in front of
you, you could not hide it, it was all in your eyes and I felt beautiful
again and accepted and reassured that I could have that type of unspoken
love again which I had lost. Just the way you touched my body, you
touched me like...like I was yours...your touch felt so...familiar. I could
hear you breathing feel your heartbeat through the palms of your hands
as they glided over my skin, the attention to detail touching me softly in
spots and firm in others. You captivated my mind, body and soul without
trying. I experienced an orgasm just by your touch alone, as your hands
cupped and massaged my inner thighs I couldn't hold it, the sensation

drove me wild and I could feel the tingle from your warm hands touching me..." She turned away from me embarrassed.

"Forgive me for pouring out my heart to you in this way but you opened a door that has been closed now for so many years. Never once have you denied me the right to express myself to you and I am so happy to find you as a genuine outlet".

I interrupted her before she could finish,

"Thank you Shelly and I am truly sorry for everything that you have gone through and hope that things get better for you. And yes I will admit that this has gone far past my expertise. I am a massage therapist and I don't want to give you the wrong impression or lead you on in any way. I know what I do is very intimate and I can admit that at times I have found myself looking a little too hard at bodies, uhhmm, well you in this case, but it's normal and we are human and things that are pleasing to us we are going to look or even act on it, but to be fair this is how I eat and pay my bills so I have to have a level of professionalism. I will not deny the attraction but for business' sake. I will have to put some boundaries in place so that we both are protected and acting accordantly. Do you agree?"

She nodded her head and begins to cry again, this time even harder from feeling embarrassed that she shared her feelings with me.

The truth of the matter is just this, I can not fall in love or in lust with every beautiful woman I meet. I have a job to do and do it with integrity, not to mention I'm treading on thin ice in my practice because she can say I did something inappropriate and my ass will be going to jail. Shelly calmed down and we talked the rest of the night and I had made a new friend and unwillingly added another service to my mobile practice, and it seemed to work... I got paid for my time.

Thai

"Stretching you to your limits."

The dynamics of my job started to shift and I could see all the ways that I could move my business up and over the competition by offering the type of service that added much needed value to a practice that, in some ways, was losing ground in the new world. The shift was happening, health, food and lifestyles were now becoming the major trends and I had to refocus and rebrand. The public was well aware of the benefits of eating clean and exercise but had not fully accepted that massage was the other missing part of that formula of health. I don't know if the connotations and sexual undertones had hurt or helped my practice at all, and depending on who you spoke to each person had a different opinion all together. It was on me to oversell the benefits, do away with the stereotypes and get these folks into the mindset of taking care of their whole bodies, not just what they put inside them. It would not be easy by any stretch of the imagination.

I ran my company with no set demographic, because in my mind the more wide reaching approach was going to net me diversity, loyal customers, a greater understanding of the goal of my company, and great crossover that would lead to more money, because green was the only color I cared about. Variety was the name of the game and I had to be versatile in my approach and marketing to get to know my potential customers. It was merely on the specific campaign that I was running that month. Like I said, it was wide and my dragnet was diverse. You could find me uptown one day or in the hood the next. I was fortunate enough to be invited out to a company health fair initiative; they were doing health screenings and each employee could qualify for a lower cost or a reduction in their health care premium.

To qualify, they had to do two things: have better numbers on their charts than the previous year, or have a health care plan they were following to garner better health, a diet plan, an exercise program, or life change geared towards an overall healthier life style. That's where I came into the equation. Health benefits from massage are historically noted and just simple you would think, right? Nope! Still the consensus was that all we do is 'rubbing,' make you feel good, then after that you're back to your normal day to day. They had no idea of the model of manipulation of soft tissue and how real the results were and how beneficial it can be in their lives.

Once I was setup at the venue, I barely got any looks; they would walk by my table look and keep going. The nerve of this guy to be here trying to get his rocks off by rubbing on us. I can't make this up, cause people are just that dumb and uninformed. At the health fair, I kid you not, I only had two people come up and speak to me about the benefits of massage and only one allowed me to do a demo for them in the massage chair. Tough crowd to win over, for sure, but they did offer me a time slot every Wednesday to come up to the offices and do ten minute massages for the employees. Problem was, it was a gamble, every employee was responsible for paying me directly for my services and there were no guarantees on the money or who would show up. I made a commitment for at least two Wednesdays but the first day was a loss, no one showed up.

Prior to the next Wednesday I called the office and asked if I could send out some informative material that would help push the employees in the right direction. That was approved, so I had them sent and distributed to all at this particular office. In my write-up I asked specific questions that would interest office workers; "How do you deal with stress? At the end of your work day, work week, do you feel tired, discomfort? What's your disposition?"

Somewhere in there I was able to get them to at least make the questionnaires mandatory and the massage optional. It worked, the following Wednesday was packed! Now I was in a position to take my company to the next level. I figured with the amount of employees they had in that building alone would be more than enough. For the next two months, every Wednesday I was booked, so I made myself available that whole work day. Some would come in the morning, or around lunch, or an hour right before their shift ended. I used my wit and charm to woo more employees to come, get a chair massage and learn more about the benefits of massage. I had a pretty even bunch of men and women, young and old, which interacted with me on Wednesdays; most times it was more Q&A. They were becoming more informed about what services I provided. With knowledge came power! I felt real good about the progress that we were making, my company and my current clients.

This was Corporate America, most of my new clients were making well into six figures and I had to turn down request for extra services outside of what their employer had already contracted me out for. I refused conflicts of interest, but again that didn't stop them from trying. I was invited to the company-wide Christmas party, not to work but as a guest. I had built a good rapport with the staff and other employees, so I accepted the offer. By now we all were on a first name basis and I was just like one of them. I learned a lot about investment bankers, the lingo and financial jargon; more than diversifying my portfolio, they were just like any other persons except being more than able to support their expensive habits. I have always been a great judge of character so reading people's true intentions came with the territory; you don't miss the part of being in tune with body language when you deal with bodies all the time, so I was well-versed.

I was the proverbial fly on the wall. I was able to see everything and hear everything. Now I had gone to quite a few parties, gotten real comfortable with folks high up on the food chain, and it got real interesting. Parties always bring out the wild side of people and alcohol makes them talk and do things they normally wouldn't do without the liquid courage. It was pretty much like all the rest of the parties I had attended, very quiet and dry, I overhead one of the executives saying

"This year's party is gonna be off the chain! I will make sure that we have maximum attendance and whoever misses it will regret that they did." John was a newly elected official with the company and his predecessor was 'An Old Fart' as Melissa in Futures called him.

The younger more charismatic John was going to show a new and fresh face for the company. I tell you this, he was not lying; it was off the muthafucking chain! First off, I was there early, I believe in being on time so I made it there fashionably prompt in anticipation for "The Party of the Year" quote end quote. It started off like how all the parties were but they changed the rules this year. For some reason they suggested that once you entered the party, to do your best not to leave; there was an emphasis on staying put during the course of the night and that they would not allow reentry. That was something new which had the water cooler crew buzzing. They were extra chatty at this party. They were probably wondering, just like me, what in the world did John have planned with a closed door policy? I couldn't wait to see these folks make fools of themselves. You see, I don't drink and would be the only sober soul in the party.

The party started off with a bang! A big birthday cake rolled onto the center of the dance floor and out pops this shirtless man and busting out from another section of the cake was a topless female. Now John said it was gonna be off the chain, but damn, I did not see this coming at all! This caused an uproar on the dance floor and you could tell real quick which ones were happy and who weren't. There was a stampede in two directions, one for the exit and the other towards the other side of the ballroom heading towards the roped off area. I'm always up for a good show, so I followed the crowd. Once I reached the entrance to the roped off area I couldn't believe my eyes. There were just about the same amount of people behind the roped area as there were still left from the ballroom dance floor and they were all naked! I watched as naked bodies bounced around on a large trampoline, some in a large hot tub setup in the corner and others were smoking as the rest we're having sex on a section blocked off with giant beds.

This was wild! I hadn't seen any thing like this in my life and was definitely not thinking that these professionals would be into something like this, but I guess you can't read a book by its cover. The ring leader John was in one of the beds having sex with Melissa from Futures, while a very familiar body was dancing on a table behind them.

"I know that's not who I think it is!" I said to myself, and yes, it was Shelly!

When our eyes met once again we were caught in a trance, she tried to put her head down and look away but it was too late. I walked through the room full of sex orgies and drugs until I reached her at the table that she was dancing on. She tried looking away but it was too late. I knew it was her and was surprised that she would be here dancing on a table. When I got her attention she looked like she was high as a kite, her eyes were watery and she took some time to focus on me and realize just who I was.

"Paul? Ahh damn! What are you doing here?"

"That's what I was gonna ask you!"

She motioned for me to follow her into a private room. I followed; watching as her hips bounced from side to side, her head tilted upward revealing that familiar neck line. I could feel my penis stiffening, imagining touching her again. I had not spoken to Shelly since the last time she received a massage from me, three weeks ago. I just chalked it up as a loss and could understand why she would go ghost. Whenever someone divulges a part of themselves to a perfectly normal stranger, sometimes there is remorse; they feel real shitty about it. They're embarrassed that they let their guards down and shared their deepest secrets and can never face that person again. In this case there was no difference. Not hearing from Shelly for a week, then going on three, I figured I caught her at a vulnerable time in her life and would never see or speak to her again. This was definitely a surprise and somewhat out of character I guess, but let me take that back. I didn't know her that well, so hey, anything is possible. They say watch out for the quiet ones because they are the wild ones.

As my thoughts raced through my mind, we entered a dark room which had a large bed in it that was exposed by the open window that let in the moonlight, guiding us through the dark room. I started to speak, or basically throw some much needed questions to Shelly, but right then she turns around grabs me and falls back on to the bed, dragging me on top of her. I had a notion that we were gonna go to this room to talk, explain the situation. Sex was the furthest thing from my mind…Naw, it was the only thing on my mind. I couldn't get my clothes off fast enough. No words were exchanged between me and Shelly. Night had become day and we were still at it, the music had stopped playing hours ago, the sounds of couples, singles engaged in orgies had subsided, and we were still going strong. The sun had replaced the moon's cool light from the night before and its rays were deeply penetrating my skin. My back being superheated, along with my constant movement, brought a continuous stream of sweat down my back, legs and face. Shelly looked absolutely beautiful in any light and was completely angelic at that moment. We both climaxed again and this would be our very last one. The rumble in my loins predicted a great surge of energy and depletion of all of my reserve and most potent seed; one last time and I'm completely exhausted. Laying there beside Shelly, we both breathed heavily and looked towards the bay window as the sun warmed our skin.

I had so many questions, but I choose to remain silent and let it come from her. So I waited.

She got up, headed to the restroom and motioned me to join her. We took our shower, still in complete silence, soaping each other's backs and taking turns under the shower head to rinse away the shampoo and soap from our heads.

It felt strange enough that I ended up at the freakiest office party of the year; but who would've ever thought that I would see one of my clients here, have sex for 7 hours, shower, and not even utter a damn word!

Out of the shower, we walked back to the room. She bent over picking up her clothes and I go in again. Touching her, pleasing her and entering her again. Then my mind started racing and putting things together...

"Fuck!" I yelled out, Small fucking world!"

Shelly jumped a little as we both fell to the bed, her legs shaking as my penis lay on her inner thigh. She looked back at me with a puzzled look on her face. I had figured, or at least I made the connection right away. Shelly is a lawyer who tries to bailout these corporate types, big time investors and financial planners. The company that I worked for every Wednesday and now throughout the week were Investment Bankers!

I sat there trying to figure out the next thing that was gonna come out my mouth; sure enough it's kinda too late to ask her about her dealings with these freaks, because lo and behold she is one of them!

But damn, how long? And damn, I'm normally a good judge of character. I really didn't see the freak in her. I started to speak, and then she stopped me.

"Look, I'm sorry for not telling you, hell who would have thought we would ever see each other again and like this. The day at the mall was a fluke, I'm never at the mall, just decided that day to go pick up my favorite comfort food."

I interrupted, "Yeah, a cheese cake concrete with honey roasted peanuts sprinkled on top. Funny thing is, now it's my favorite; I tried it out and fell...

"In love," we both said in unison.

I couldn't believe it but the connection that we were building was evident, way past the emotional and physical, mentally we were starting to connect. I admit that I was all business before meeting Shelly. I could give a rat's ass about my customers, just get the massage, don't talk, give me my money and I'm off. I understood the part that she explained during our first talk, that massage was very intimate and there had to be some thought about expanding my thought process and welcoming conversations with my clients, because it was a release for them and they would feel more comfortable with me. I was tethering on something dangerous, I had never thought to ever do, have sex with my client. That's how I still saw Shelly, even after we had sex, and I broke my golden rule: "Never mix business and Pleasure." That was what I stood on. I took my practice very seriously, not to wind up here... Damn!

"Hey! Hey! Snap out of it!" Shelly yelled at me as she pushed me back on the bed.

"Listen...I just can't."

"I know what's on your mind, you are now stressing out about going against your rules and professionalism," she said, using her hands and fingers to put emphasis on her air quotes. "Have you ever thought that Pleasure is a Business? Tell me something... on average how many clients are you getting per day or per month?"

I tried to answer but she just kept talking, putting a finger up to my lips as if to say, 'Don't answer yet.'

"Do they really help pay all of your bills? What makes you better than the next therapist? You're good... damn good," she said as she bit her bottom lip and laid back on the bed next to me.

"You have potential for making real good money but you may have to relax some of your textbook bullshit. This is real world shit and peddling a massage to 'manipulate soft tissue' not going to cut it and I doubt if anyone knows what that all means or even cares about."

I answered defensively, "Well, I do well for myself and I have... well, had a great contract."

"You have a gift. I just hate to know you are working yourself to death, and not even enjoying your job."

"Sound familiar to me!" As I directed the pun to her pushing her on her shoulder, she smiled.

"Look, I understand what you are saying; I try to stay professional and this...damn I really fucked up, I don't mix business and pleasure."

"Paul, I know, I've heard your song and dance, 'I don't do that I don't do this' I get that!" Shelly looked at me waving her hands side to side to side in a childish manner. "I'm just saying that you would make more money if you went by my suggestion."

"And what would that be exactly?"

"Make Pleasure your Business. You've done well by me and I have enjoyed every minute of it."

"That was definitely not my intention. I gave you a massage, didn't do anything else...until now. And actually this doesn't count because I was not working."

The more I was explaining myself, the more I knew she was not buying my explanation at all. She had her mind set on what happened. I had gone against my rules and ethics and felt bad about my decision. I'm human right? I had a weak moment. I sat there thinking about what happened.

"Hey! Well, I got to go, I had a great time. Hopefully this is not gonna ruin our business relationship. Can I still get massages from you? Strictly professional, ok?"

I hesitated as the gravity of what was going on hit me. Damn, she could flip on me, turn this shit into something different; she's a lawyer so she could twist it and get me in real trouble. I'm attracted to her and can't hide the fact that I am. The thought about massaging her again is gonna lead to just sex; I know I won't be able to do just that after having this freaky night with her. Damn! I run my business in a way that I don't end up in this type of situation. I have to avoid her at all costs!

"Yeah...yeah we can do that," I responded half-heartedly, knowing my plan was to never see her ass again.

Shelly left the room. I got dressed and started to head out of the room. As I put my shoes on, I could hear John's voice, he was yelling something loudly and some other people in the back ground started chanting also.

"Good morning!! Whew! What a fucking night!"

His voice started to get closer and I could hear him kicking doors open, coming closer to my door. I stood up and opened the door.

He yelled out, "Touchy Feely!" the name that he gave me the day he hired me to work for the company.

He embraced me and shook my hand. "How are you doing? Long night? Well I need you to do some work for us today; we have some sore ladies if you know what I'm saying! I've got the guys covered with another massage therapist. Hey Shelly! Come here!"

What? Shelly is the other therapist?! Fuck! I knew she had to be, having her massage table at her house. Damn! I thought to myself.

"Hey John..." I started to speak, but he ignored me.

"Shelly, are we going to be good in court? You know just in case the stiffs' wanna go to court and cry to the judge about our party?"

"No we are gonna be fine, I have it all covered. I'm heading out to meet with the judge by 2pm today. Ok, gotta run, talk to you later." She winked at me, as she walked across the room.

"That's fucking fantastic Shelly! You my Nig...Can I say it please?" She nods her head and he continues." You my Nigga! Ugh ahh yeah!!"

There was an awkward silence in the hall while the other people watched, shocked and waiting on my response. I just nervously laughed off the comment, I was still processing everything.

She stopped and turned around at the door saying, "John don't work him too hard, he still needs to have enough energy for me later on."

"No problem, we will take good care of him!" He yelled as he smacked my back.

Shelly waved goodbye and closed the door behind her. Man, my mind was racing, my heart was pounding. I really thought that she was the other therapist. I had mixed emotions about continuing doing any more massages, so I started to head out of the room. I headed across the hall leading to the ballroom and heading towards the elevators. Then John came running behind me.

"Hey, I forgot." He reached into his pocket, pulled out a check and handed it to me. "Just wanted to give you a bonus and thank you for all the work you have done for us. It really has helped with the team; they are all more relaxed now and focused, business is better since you have been here. Thank you."

"Thank you, sir, I did have a good time and didn't really get any sleep last night so..." John interjected,

"Yeah, I know it was a wild night! Don't worry, go home and get some sleep; rest up, cause I'ma need you to be fresh and ready. Here is the address where you will be working tonight."

He gave me an envelope with a yellow piece of paper in it, and a shit load of cash. It looked like at least a couple thousand dollars. I took the envelope and began to speak.

"Hey!" John yelled, and pulled me in. He whispered, "Welcome aboard. Get you some rest and see you later tonight."

Damn, he didn't even give me a chance to explain. I had clients already booked for the rest of the week and was gonna be past exhausted. On my way down in the elevator, I opened the check up and saw that it was a company check. Normally I was paid directly into my account, never by check. The check had my full name, home address, tax info and year to date, showing $82,000! I was more than shocked; I almost fainted seeing that type of money for a couple months of work. I knew that there had to be a catch to it but I couldn't just abandon my clients, so I called them to see if I could schedule earlier appointments. They all agreed.

I pride myself in being professional and making sure that I took an approach based on my customers' needs; my clients have multiple issues and I would not feel right excusing them. Mrs. Peters works in property management and the stress of the job has gotten to her. Long hours and a heavy workload caused her to have a stroke. She had been to the doctors and they have been giving her shock therapy, but it was very painful and she could not see any results, other than associating pain with the therapy and agonizing over the next appointment. We met one day while I was out at a health fair that was set up by the community center near where I lived. I noticed her and could see that she was in a lot of pain as she tried to walk up the stairs entering the complex.

"Hello, can I help you?" As I reached my arm out to help assist her up the stairs.

"Thank you so much. I am here to get a massage and have some questions answered, I have been going through shock therapy for the last three weeks and it is not helping at all. It seems to be hurting more than helping."

"Well I'm glad that you are here and I hope that I can help you and answer any questions that you may have."

She looked at me and smiled, I could tell that she had recently suffered a stroke. The left side of her face was drooping and her speech was sort of slurred. Once she was on my table, I noticed that she was very sensitive to touch; just about everything that I did hurt her. So I started off with light stretching and very light massage and energy work.

She was more than pleased with the results of the reflexology session that she became a regular customer, I have been seeing her now for the last four months. Her condition has gotten better; no longer is she suffering from the stroke-like symptoms; her face has straightened out and her mobility has progressed. Her legs, arms and flexibility with her back and waist have dramatically improved. She is about 80% normal. I had a commitment to my clients and that was priority one.

I met with Mrs. Peters at her home when she had just come back from water therapy and swim class. We've built a great friendship over the time that we have known each other and have grown fond of one another. We have shared just about everything that has gone on with our lives, family, relationships, ups and downs. It's funny because when I look back at how I managed myself and business I always wanted to separate the business and personal aspects of massage to keep what I thought of as a professional relationship. But I'm now seeing where there is a level of intimacy. It develops when you spend time getting to know the client.

"Paul! Nice to see you again! How has your week been? Happy Holidays. How is your family? And you?"

"I'm doing good, Mrs. Peters."

"Come on now, we are no longer formal, it's Janet. I'm only a year older than you, so stop that with the Mrs. it's Ms. and only Janet. Got it? Good!"

I agreed and hung my head for a minute trying to figure out just how I was going to tell her about my crazy week.

"Well, I fucked up royally! Remember how when we first met I told you that I separated business from pleasure? Well I actually had sex with one of my clients last night."

"Ahh damn! Give me the juice! I need details, baby! I told you one day you was gonna crack! I know you see a lot of naked bodies but you can't resist them all!"

"Naw, it wasn't even like that. I did the massage weeks ago and then I was invited to this office party; you know, the bankers, investors I work for threw a wild party last night, it was crazy."

"O my damn, they turned you out?!" Janet started giggling to herself uncontrollably.

"The new owner is a freak! He told everybody it was gonna be a closed door party and shit! I saw why. The party started off just like other parties and a normal white collar office party, you know water cooler chatting and drinks, but then it was taken to 'A Whole Nother 'evel' I mean strippers, drinks, drugs, hot tubs and fucking orgies! I couldn't believe my eyes, you had folks tryna get out of the place and folks running to the big beds where naked bodies were slamming against each other and dancers on poles, fog machines, lights the whole nine!"

"Wait! Wait! Wait! What?! You mean to tell me that you went to a swingers club?"

"No it was a Christmas office party at a hotel!"

"Poor Paul sweetie! Did they take your virginity? She jumps off the table and rolls around on the floor losing her towel fully naked laughing.

"Yes sounds like you were invited to a Swingers event! Now what happened with you and having sex with your client?"

"Ok I'm getting to that...so I was sipping on my soda or at least I thought it was just soda, because you know me I don't drink. Out of nowhere comes this big ass cake on wheels. A naked man and woman jump out of it. The wall or curtain moves and John, the new CEO, starts yelling and running and jumps in the bed with a group of naked women. Then through the crowd of people I saw a familiar body and it was my client."

"What? Wait you can pick a body out of a lineup? Lol she must have a body to remember!"

"I knew it was her; we only saw each other no more than three times ever but I spent enough time with her to know that was her. The curve of her cheek bones and how pronounced her masseter and risorius were causing her orbicularis oris to draw back...."

"English Gotdamnit man!!! You can really fuck up a wet dream. Damn!"

"Well, the shape of her face, she has a really nice face and her full lips complimented her face and she was just sexy as hell."

"Well that's what you should have said damnit!"

"I did."

"No you didn't with all that medical mumbo jumbo. Ok so what happened next?"

"Ok so I saw her and she was just dancing. I approached her, she tried to hide a little and she pulled me into a room. We had sex and showered, had sex again, then she left and the boss man gave me this." I pulled out the check and envelope filled with money and handed it to Janet.

"Damn! Pleasure is a business that pays well! So they paid you for having sex with her?"

"No this was my bonus money and I guess pay for the rest of the year, but look at the amount!"

"Yeah 82 Grand! Now that is scary! What else they want you to do for them? Hide a body or something? Hell are they hiring? I need a paycheck like this!"

"I don't know but it's crazy. I go to school to learn massage as a profession, to be professional and help people with their problems. I never thought it would be like this."

"Look I know you are having a hard time with this but you are still a professional and I doubt anyone is gonna call the police on you and have you locked up for doing what you did. Hell, that's what they wanted anyway! They're going to pay you good money for those hands and pole lol!"

"They want me to come back tonight to work a party again, I didn't get a chance to tell John that I'm not gonna be able to make it because I am dead tired and I had plans today to take care of my clients first."

"Ahh, that's so sweet, but you dumb as shit! If it was me I would call all my customers and let them know like this. 'Hello...yes, this is Paul and I ain't never coming back! Lol, so when are you gonna tell him you are not going to make it?"

"I'm not, I'm going to send my friend Daniel to do the party; it won't matter because they will have someone there and it will all work out"

"I hope it don't backfire on you. Well, give me one of those fantasy massages you gave her and maybe I will luck up and have me a swinger's party of my own!"

I called Daniel after I finished my massage with Janet, then rescheduled the other massages I had for the day. Daniel came over to pick up an extra table from me for the party. John sent me a text and mentioned that the party was starting earlier than planned and left me the directions to the place. I paid Daniel for taking over the party for me and helped him get the tables into his truck. I was so exhausted I took a shower and went straight to bed.

Aromatherapy

"My plan had been rewritten over and over again and now I had a new one which had my nose wide open."

The next morning I'm awakened by a constant ringing. It's my doorbell and cell phone going off at the same time and who's ever at my door really needs to get in. I get up and see that I've got 26 missed calls, 21 of them from Shelly, 2 from my mom, 2 from Daniel and 1 from John. I dial John as I walk to my front door to open it, its Daniel pacing at the door smiling.

"Good morning."

"You mean afternoon my dude! Damn you slept all night and day? Look I gotta thank you for last night!"

wave my hand to let him know that the call picked up.

"Good afternoon!" John yells on the other end of the phone. "Look here guy..."

Damn! I thought to myself this can't be good. I sent Daniel to the party and didn't tell him, I'm sure he is pissed.

"Whoever your partner is, I wanna kiss the motherfucker myself! got word back from my new clients and the show he put on last night was perfect! The ladies really enjoyed themselves and the divorcee really had a great time, if you know what I mean. Look, I knew you were tired and you didn't have to tell me, but you made a great call on this one and that's why I pay you the big bucks, kid. You really know your stuff. Just wanted to thank you and tomorrow night let's celebrate. Later!"

"Ohh ok, cool I'm glad everything worked out." John hangs up the phone in mid-sentence.

Daniel has made himself something to eat and is sitting on my couch with his legs up, eating, watching the game and sipping on a beer. I'm just still trying to clear my mind and wake up.

"Dude! I love you man!"

Daniel jumps up and hugs me, then reaches into his pocket pulling out two rubber band stacks of cash.

"Here you go! Thanks for getting me that job, it's been hard out here lately and you came up on a lick and shared it with a brotha!"

Daniel was one of my massage classmates from California. He started school a week after I started and always bragged about what he was gonna do once he got certified as a massage therapist. He was the kid in class that always had something to say.

"Damn! Dawg, look how phat she is! Would you hit that? Yeah you wouldn't know what to do with that!"

I was born and raised in Upstate New York and my father ran a physical therapy practice and my mom is a chiropractor, so me being a massage therapist wasn't too far off the path they wanted for me. They actually wanted me to go to med school to be a surgeon. Close enough, I guess. I upheld all the things that were required of me being compliant with the laws, HIPPA, professionalism and just decency. Some of my classmates could care less and Daniel was one of them. He used massage school just to add to his repertoire of 'getting bitches,' so any and everything he learned was gonna be just another way to seduce and conquer. I looked down at the roll of cash neatly held together with a thick rubber band and it seemed to be way more than I paid him for taking the job.

We agreed I would just take a third of what he made in tips, because I knew how much he really needed the money. We were almost ten years Outta School, and trying to keep your businesses consistant was tough, so it was tough times for a lot of folks.

"There you go my Brotha, 3 stacks for you!"

"What the hell!? Damn D, did you rob them?!"

"Naw, my dude, no robbery at all, it was...a Fuckfest Bae-beee!"

He jumped on my couch screaming and yelling and I couldn't understand; not one word! He just kept swearing and laughing, doing motions like he was humping the recliner back and forth, then began to throw the money from his pockets up in the air. Once he settled down he shook my hand again and patted me on my back.

"Look...let me tell you what happened, my dude"

He was exhausted and out of breath. He tried another sip of his beer but it was empty so he cracked open another one and took a big chug. Wiping his mouth and taking a deep breath he starts his story,

"That party was a divorce party with like 30 fine ass bitches up in there! I took my time to set up the tables then some crazy white dude came through, asking about you and I told him that I was there working for you and he asked me,

'Kidd, can you handle this?'

"Man you know me!? I was like, 'Yeah I'm game, no problem.'

"My dude, I was thinking about all the time I used to tell ya'll in class about how many bitches I was getting from learning this massage thing and I was partly lying a little. I had at lease two that rode for me real strong though, but these bitches they were ready! So while I'm setting up, the dude just sitting back lolly-gagging and talking business to the ladies getting divorced, right. And she peeping me out and shit, so you know me, I'm like playing it cool cause I can't let her see me sweat, ya dig? Gotta keep it professional-like and shit. So I act like I was doing my thing setting up and getting ready. I'm G'd down, got my scrubs on wit them custom Jays, you know how I do it, grey on grey joints nobody got them yet Tony hooked me up wit them last week and you know he customize the scrubs too. You need to holla at him and get your shits from him. Well, back to what happen right... so party going and white dude leaving and shit so he slide me a couple bills and whispers to me,

'Don't fuck this up homeboy.'

"I held that shit tho. It took everything in me not to smack the fucking taste out of his mouth! That's on my G'MA for real for real. So I'm like,

'Bet. I will make sure the lovely ladies enjoy their time tonight.'

All proper-like and shit so he wouldn't sweat me. So he was like,

'I'm out G!'

"Now I didn't know if your boy was stupid or something, but I ain't take too kind to this dude try'n me for one, talk all fly and shit to me then gonna act like he cool and shit talking about 'I'm out G!' Man, I wish he would...but I snapped outta it real fast when he slid me a couple more bills. He must've seen the expression on my face. Straight Murda! Hahahaa! Ok, so back to it, right. Well, I'ma put it in terms that you might be more comfortable wit cause I think I'm losing you on my grammar, lol. You always cut us up about the way we talk so I'ma show you some versatility."

"Yes, let's try the versatility, minus all the other bullshit and see if I can follow you."

"My dude, let's not get it twisted up in this bitch. Because I speak a certain way don't mean I can't get wit your proper speaking, bland food eating ass!"

"Alright! I got your point so tell me about the party."

"Alright, so here it is, let me draw the picture for you real quick. It's a party, 30 sexy females and one of me, sexy chocolate specimen, muscular build, square shoulders, broad chest, strong back, legs, hands of a god, male member envy of the world, yes I'm packing, standing 6'3"."

"Ok Mandingo, are you ever gonna get to what happened?"

"Ok so here we go:

"So after my exchange with John, who I assumed was the proprietor of the company that originally hired you for the job that you passed on to me, I felt more inspired to do my best because I had five hundred dollars of tax free money sitting in my left pocket. The night started off in the right direction. The ladies did what they came to do and that was party. They were celebrating the end of a long relationship between the divorcee and the terrible husband. She had known him for three long months before marrying him and spent an agonizing 21 months of being all alone in his big house, traveling the world alone as he worked and travelled the world without her, only meeting with her on weekends at any determined island in the world, and from the looks of it she was sick of it and called her lawyer and her financial adviser to plan the divorce.

Sounded crazy to me but who am I to judge. For the last two years, her and 29 of her closet friends traveled the world, becoming jet setters, having to travel the whole world twice and it became a bore to them, not having what she wanted the most, companionship and understanding from the man she loved. She needed more time with him and he didn't understand. Why did he need to work all those hours and meet her in

London on Tuesdays for tea time? Why couldn't they lay in bed more like every Friday in Dubai, staring out at their panoramic view from the 65th floor, gazing at Atlantis as fireworks explode in the distance? She was fed up and wanted, no needed, a divorce from her husband...

Yeah that's the story I heard from the majority of the half-naked and shit faced women at the party. My dude, I was saying to myself, 'Damn this a dumb ass bitch,' but with all the liquored up women around me and how fine they was, not to mention the money I had in my pocket, who was I to judge? Yeah, the nerve of this man to work and give her and her friends all of this and not enough time.

Ok so back to the heart of this story. So as the night goes on every one is dancing, the DJ is playing jams back to back and it's just me and 30 ladies. I have the table setup and ready, the bartender ask me what I'm drinking, so I said water cause I didn't want to 'fuck up' cause you know me and liquor is not a good combo especially around these fine ass ladies."

"OK, get to the point already!"

"So I got paper in my pocket. I'm feeling good. I kill the first cup of water quick, then ask for another one and by that time I get my first client. She all drunk and touchy feely, asking me how do I want her to lay on the table, and I said on her stomach so I can massage her back. Now the music is pumping so you can hardly hear yourself think, so every time I speak to one of the ladies I have to be damn near screaming or in their ear. So I start the massage and she goes to sleep like that! Lol, slobbering and snoring, you could hear her even wit the music playing. So I had four tables set up, so I went to the next table and started massaging the next woman, which was the divorcee. She immediately took off all her clothes and whispered to me that she always gets a massage with a happy ending. Well, you know me, I had to act like you and be professional, thinking about what your boss said, 'Don't Fuck

Up,' so I was gonna play it cool no matter what came out of these drunk women's mouths.

The bartender sent another water over to me. By this time I'm sweating a little from the massage; she requested deep tissue and I was really working up a sweat. I figured the damn bartender slipped me something in my drink but when I looked down at my arm I saw a crazy stamp on my forearm and I hadn't seen it on there before. It was yellow and white with a picture of a rhino on it. I peeled it off and threw it in the trash. By that time most of the women from the party were in the section where all the tables were set up, just watching as I massaged the woman of the hour. They kept pinching my butt and blowing kisses at me.

I felt a little drunk at that point and everything started to feel and look weird. I think that patch was some kind of drug because I started to just feel real airy in the head. I looked down and the divorcee has my dick in her mouth. The ladies started to gather around and cheering her on, which made her turn up even more. Now you know me, homeboy, it's ok to get my Jimmy wet but I don't navigate strange dark alleys without my hinna, so you know I got to stay strapped, so I pushed her off me and grabbed for my bag. She pulled me back over to the table and another woman pushed me down as she pulled a condom out of its wrapper, put it in her mouth and began to work it down my dick. Now they all around rubbing on me and making me touch them. Once the condom was fully on, the divorcee jumps right on up on the table and straddles me and it's on! She is bucking wildly as I can feel my fingers being sucked by two other women and they have taken off all my clothes. Man, I'm butt-ball naked. I can even feel them rubbing their pussy on my feet! I think one of them was tryna get my whole foot in her! Whatever they gave me started to kick in, cause all I could remember is just the feeling of her riding me and hearing the music blasting in my ears.

When I woke up the next morning it was another group of women's turn. I had sobered up from that drug they gave me and was ready to fuck some more, I fucked about 12 more this morning before I showered and got over to your house. The divorcee joined me in the shower and we fucked some more, she told me her name was Tasha and she wanted to see me again without all of her friends.

My dude! Thank you for getting me this gig, it had to be by far the best thing to ever happen to me ever and you know I needed that money so bad too! It's hard as hell out here trying to make a living off of this textbook promoting like you. I guess you got the complexion for the connection."

"Well I don't have the complexion for the connection, whatever that means, I just go out there and pass out cards every day at the mall and did little demos and started to build up my clients that way. I just lucked up on getting that job with the investment bankers, day trader freaks, whatever they do. I guess they all are freaks, huh."

"You damn right they freaks and we been going about this whole thing wrong!"

"Why would you say that?"

"Because Pleasure is a Business baby! And we losing out if we don't take advantage of the pleasure part of this business and it seems like we could make way more money in Pleasure than "Professionalism" as he uses his fingers with air quotes.

"That's funny because I heard that saying before..."

"Yeah my dude, it's real out here and money to be made, but I know you ain't never gonna walk on the wild side anyway so I'm wasting my breath talking to you."

"That's not true...I have walked on the wild side"

"What!? You? Really? For real? You was wit one of those freaks also? What happened?"

"Well, I went to the Christmas Party the company threw and wind up seeing a client of mine and we spent the night together."

"So did you fuck!?"

"Yes we had sex."

"Yes we had sex. Lol. Damn! My dude got his dick wet! No bullshit? Wow!"

"Yeah, it really wasn't supposed to happen; saw her at the party and it happened. And I'm questioning my duty to this profession, my clients, hell my parents, that make a good living doing the right thing and not involving themselves with their clients and definitely not sleeping with them, I really fucked up."

"Man look at it this way they wanted it, it wasn't like you came at her with it; you stayed professional and she made the pass at you. And I know you probably gave her a disclaimer and bullshit and she ain't care about none of it and just wanted the dick! Lol!"

"Yeah but that's not what I do for a living I…"

"I know you. 'Manipulate Soft Tissue!'" He injected before I could finish.

"Blah blah blah blah… we live in the real world and truth be told just because we are certified and running a business out here it doesn't mean we are guaranteed clients, money or success. Find your lane my dude. Money can be made out here, it's just how you go about making it happen using the skills you developed and learned from school and it might work for you and maybe it won't. I'm trying everything!"

"Well that's good for you. I will do my best not to get caught up."

Daniel left after he finished his six pack and the phone started ringing again.

Reflexology

"Cause and effect, your deliberate strokes deliver an equal and accurate reaction."

"Hello. May I speak to Paul?"

"Yes, Paul speaking, may I help you?"

"Hey Paul its Chase...do you remember me? We went to school together and I went to night school with you."

I had originally started going to school during the day, but then I got a job so I switched to nights with only three months left. I didn't really remember a lot of folks from night school because, to be honest, I was just trying to get it over with. The schedule of working all day then school at night was wearing on me and I was almost half asleep most of the time in school at night.

"Uhm, yeah I think I remember you..."

"Yeah, I hung out with Megan and Tish, remember them?"

"Ohh yeah, now I do! Cool! How are you doing?"

"I'm doing...I got your number from Megan. She said that you were the person to call. You know it's been rough out here lately. I had my own shop open for about 7 years but I had to close it because it had become too damn expensive; client list had dropped over the years, the rent alone was just way too high, you know."

While he is talking I am still trying to figure out just exactly who he is, because a lot of people went by nicknames and I hardly ever knew anyone's actual real name. Chase, now I remember him, or her, as Megan and Tish would say. A very nice guy and kept the class always laughing. Chase had a wealth of information when it came to massage; he was one of the classmates that I would listen to when it came to situational therapy. See, I'm a thinker, and I think outside the box and pattern my approach to massage in that way, 'What-ifs and Solutions.' He had it all figured out and his slogan was, 'There's a massage for that' and there really was. For any condition and aliment he could find some type of massage that would be beneficial. I was just wondering how he got my number and why.

"Megan said word around town is that you are the man out here doing the mobile massage gig, so please fill me in on what you're doing and how it's sticking, because, hunti, it has dried up out here. Maybe you have all the answers and clients and I wanna know how can I be down."

I could visualize him doing a hair flip for hair that's not even there.

"Chase it's been about the same with me too, other than this one contract I have that is keeping me afloat. And it hasn't come without plenty of surprises, I'm really rethinking this whole profession, just some things I don't do, but it seems like its drawing me in and having me to choose between my morals and making a buck."

"Yas, hunti, I know what you mean cause I'm about to lose my religion! Shooot! I've had my own issues to deal with; it's just hard to get good decent clients that know how beneficial massage can be in their lives."

"Thank you, Chase! I deal with that all the time, trying to change the culture and having people understand that we don't just rub on folks and we are qualified in treating the human body."

"Yaas, but you got to change these folks' minds before we even get to getting them on your table and breaking bread with you."

"Sounds like you have been having the same issues like me huh?"

"Ewe girl, bye! You don't even know the half! I really want to partner up with someone so it will be safer for me and we can combine our companies, or have an investor to help, so I could step away from this completely on the work side and hire some therapist to do the work. When I tell you it's been crazy, it has been cauh-raayzeey, hunti!"

"I figured that you wouldn't really have a problem here in Atlanta since you know..."

"No, fuck that Paulie; don't start that shit with me. Paaaauuuul ok! Hmm shhmpop! Just cause I like mens and they like my fine ass don't mean I'm gonna cash in on all of them. Hell we go through the same shit you do, even worse! So you straight, so do you have women and straight men knocking down your door to get a massage huh? Huh! Answer that! I'll wait! Negative! So don't give me that shit! And since we on the subject I gotta tell you about this one client that has been buggin the mess outta me to give him a massage; you know me and money go well, child. But he can keep his money cause I ain't the one!"

"What's the problem with him?"

"Bih! Shid! What's not... the problem? A fucking bugaboo that's the problem, a fake ass, frontin', down low Brotha and he's a big time athlete too! Emmhumph! Yeah you heard me right, a big time one who be frontin' for his boys but if they only knew!"

"Well that sounds like a handful. Why not just avoid him, call the police if he is harassing you like that."

"Well at first I was not bothered at all when he first made the comments but....well this how it all happened:

A week after dismantling my business at the shop, I started promoting my mobile company. I did a lot of stuff in the paper, radio and even did that little commercial spot. You know the one that came on at halftime at the Hawks game and for every home game I got my 15 seconds of fame and that was not cheap at all! I damn near went broke trying to keep up wit the Jones bae-bae for real! For the love of God I don't know why I did that; it seemed like I just brought it on myself and it came in the package of this over-zealous asshole. He is a football player who bugged the shit outta me and even assaulted me. So this is what happened, so I'm at the airport, hustling, really breaking the law, cause you know damn well them folks don't allow you to post up and advertise there, period, without having a booth there or something, hunti! I ain't had license or permit the first! Just out there passing out cards and offering chair massages to folks right there on the spot. Funny thing is they didn't even stop me; actually, security told me to go through the gates, catch the train down to Concourse A, and setup there. Yaaas hunti I was shown favor, hey bae-bae, getting that guwap! You hear me?! So I set up and as these folks waited for their flights and got off, I was working! Blessing them with the softest hands in the business and money coming off they ass like! I bust that ass for $1258 in one day, working the dollar a minute massages! That's the day I ran into this arrogant ass motherfucker! I was done doing a chair massage and taking a break eating lunch when he approached me talking about,

'So what you doing over here?'

I'm like, duh? Don't come for me! You seen me over here doing massages all day long and now you wanna come over here with a dumb ass question? You betta take your no sense of fashion ass over to Lenox and get accessorized, hunti, and get yo ass a royal jester suite cause you in the presence of a true queen! Get the fuck out my face peasant! Yasss I read em!

'Chill homie I ain't come over here for all that. I was just seeing what you was doing... So you run this company? I definitely need a massage but do you have a woman to do one for me?'

"Yeah I run it but it's just me."

'Ohh ok, no thank you then, don't need no fruity ass fingers on my shoulders ha!'

Then before I could respond, he turns to leave, then throws a piece of balled up paper into my plate with food still in it! This muthafucking asshole got me all fucked up! His bitch ass ran to his line to board his plane. He was every bit of 6' 2" built like a fucking beetle damn near ruined my lunch! I'm like Bih...ewwww you so lucky you getting on that plane don't ever let me see your ass again! I think I spoke too soon cause about two weeks later I'm at my gym working out and I go to the sauna room and yeah, you guessed it! It was his fake ass oversized Freddie Jackson wannabee and his goon squad in there taking up all the damn room. I sat over in the corner with the towel over my head trying not to be seen and minding my damn business.

They talked about errhbody like they had nothing wrong with them. The normal bullshit of how and why he or she is here, they fat; they asses need to be here to work some of that shit off. Then it begins, out of all the talk about pussy, cars, women, fat people, this oversize care bear with facial hair wanna go in on gay men. Out of five of his homeboys he is the only one pressed to speak on gay men and just bash us. Humph sound like I had a fan. I tucked my head down in my towel hoping he didn't notice me when I walked in as he kept staring the pot talking about what he would do to a gay man if he was left alone with one,

'Man I would fucking beat that faggot's ass for real! I'd beat his ass straight!'

They went on and on; then I just tuned them out and put my earphones in and kicked back and relaxed listening to my calming ocean sounds. Everyone left out and I assumed I was gonna finally have the place to myself, then he comes back in.

'Tootie Fruity Touchy Feely! I knew that was you! Small world and who think that I would run into you this way?'

'And the name is Chase and I heard you fronting for boys; it sounds like somebody got a problem with gay men, sounds to me like you have it out for them or is it that they had it out on you a few times and now you spreading your hate. You in the closet huh?'

Damn, I shouldn't have said that, because that made him mad. He lunged at me and put his hands around my neck and started choking me. I couldn't do shit; he was just so big he over-powered me and the next thing that happened shocked the shit outta me.

'Yeah I know you like that, lil bitch! You ain't got shit to say now huh, fuck you, fuck you, little bitch!'

Then it happened; he eased up from choking me, then pulled me close to him and put his lips on mine and pressed his tongue deep into my mouth, still with one hand on my throat. He kissed me passionately. I could feel his body on mine, pressing against mine, his hard dick getting more erect pushing against my stomach. It got a rise outta me and I fucking pissed on myself. He jumped back, trying to robe himself, concealing his hard dick with his hands. The door opened and some guys walked in and that's when I ran straight for the locker room, holding my piss soaked towel in my hands.

It was scary as hell and just crazy. He seems to follow me everywhere; I see him everywhere I go. I had a decent clientele at the gym but he has fucked that up. I'm calling you to see if you could help me with putting me on to what you are doing with this contract that you have."

"Damn, Chase, I'm sorry to hear that happened to you and yes, if and when things come up I will get in touch with you and tell you when and where. Actually I might be able to have you work my shift over at the headquarters this week to help you out a little. I normally work with them on Wednesdays but now I'm basically full time, and anyways, I need the time off to concentrate on my regular clients. So give me till the end of this week to work it all out for you."

"Ok. Thank you so much, I really appreciate that. Talk to you later."

"Yes, you welcome, bye."

Now that shit would have you to drinking and hard drugs! I couldn't believe that Chase had to go through that. Wow, almost getting raped by a straight guy, or is he. While going over what I just heard and trying to digest it, my phone goes off again.

"Damn! Am I ever going to get any sleep today? Hotline, how may I help you?"

"Huh? Hello, is this Paul?"

"Yes. Who is this?"

"It's me, Megan. Did Chase call you yet?"

"Yes, just got off the phone with him and you call right after I hung up with him. How is everything?"

"Wow! Well good timing I guess. Well things are just about the same, a client here and there but no steady income. I heard that you were doing well so I passed on the info to Chase. I'm sorry. Was that ok?"

"Yeah that was fine."

Then dead silence. I kind of figured she was waiting to throw her hat into the ring, since it seems like I was now 'the go to guy' so I sat there in silence just waiting to see what she would say.

"I'm...I," cutting her off before she was able to get it all out.

"I know you are in need of some more work or clients...right?"

"Uhhmmm...yes, how did you figure that I was going to bring that up?"

"Well, I just had a hunch that you would be asking because I have gotten calls from multiple ex-classmate this week and it's been about the same thing."

"Hey wait, I didn't call you so you can be condescending. Never mind!"

"I'm sorry; I didn't mean it in that way at all, just that I have had a lot of calls. And yes, to answer your original question...yes, I do have some extra work and would love to help you in any way that I can. But there are a couple of things that I have to go over with you; it just dawned on me after talking with Chase and Daniel, and helping Daniel with a job. I'm kind of second guessing everything."

"You helped Daniel's crazy ass? You are lucky he didn't get you fired! He is a sex-crazed maniac and all he is worried about is his 'Bitches.' Just a mess!"

"Well, with the clients he worked with, wouldn't mind, for sure."

"I guess... it's been real rough out here, Paul. You know, with me having the two kids and not getting any help, it has been hell. I worked for a company for a short while but with the cost of daycare and the little one being sick, I lost my job. I had to take off too many times and they said that they couldn't keep me."

"Damn, that is rough. I'm sorry."

There was another awkward silence and I could just hear her breathing on the other line. She took a deep breath.

"Paul, I had some close calls and almost got raped one time. I lost a lot of money, you know, just trying to do things by the book."

"Yes, I know, 'Manipulating Soft Tissue' we both said at the same time which made both of us laugh.

"Yes!"

"Yeah, but it seems like doing this out here on our own the rules have changed; people are always either cheap or trying to find a way to get something for nothing. After losing my job I went through a real rough spell. I had gotten down to my last and thankfully the babies weren't babies anymore, so I had one in first grade and the other in Pre-K, so they could go to school during the day to eat. I went two weeks without any money and no new clients, hell no clients at all. I put an ad out online and finally had someone to answer it.

"The ad was '2 Hr Massage for $50.' The customer said that all they had was $35 and I accepted it. It was the weekend and we only had enough food for one day left in the fridge. I had called my family and asked for help, but no one would. All I heard was, '*I wish I could help you but I just don't have it.*' Over and over again. They just didn't know how bad I needed some money and that my babies needed that money for food. You know I'm not originally from Atlanta. Just like you, we are a long way from home, so it's rough. So my client came over and I forgot one of the most important rules, to get the money first, I was just so glad to have a paying client."

"Please tell me this was not the guy that tried to rape you while your children were there!"

"No, no, no! My babies were over my neighbor's house and the only reason that he came to me is because my car was on E. I was on fumes and couldn't even drive down the street before it would have shut down."

"Ohh ok...whew!"

"Yeah, that was not the case this time. I was just ready to get the massage done and over and get my babies something to eat and at least put $5 in my gas tank to take them back and forth to school the next week. So after the massage was done, he sat there on the table and looked up at me and asked,

'So what's next?'

"Huh? What? You were done with the massage; what's next was him paying you right and going home?"

"Yes, Paul, but he wanted more than that. He pulled his boxers off and started to rub his dick looking at me."

"What!?"

"Yes, he wanted a happy ending."

"A happy ending?"

"Damn Paul, it's true what they say about you!"

"True what? What do they say about me?"

"Ahh never mind, lol, well he wanted to have sex with me!"

"Damn! And he wanted to trade sex with what he owed you in return?"

"Yes, Paul. Yes!"

"Wow that's really fucked up! Didn't he know that you really needed that money so that you and your babies could eat?"

"No, Paul, he didn't know that. It's just the point; he could care less and wanted what he wanted. I was not going to degrade myself or disrespect my kids in that way just for a little bit of money. I got real mad at that point and told him that he would pay me and go home. He looked at me crazy and gave me the money and got dressed and left out of my apartment and slammed the door. I just sat there for a while before I broke down crying. I was in a bad place and in the worst rut I had ever been in and no help from my family and no real money coming in since I lost my job and realizing that I was so close to not having any money at all to feed my kids."

"Well, how come you didn't just go downtown and apply for assistance for you and your children?"

"Well, they said I had to wait, plus I made too much to get more than just $45 from them for food assistance. $45? Who can live off of that? I had bills to pay and plus I didn't have a job anymore; they were real rude with me when I went down there. I just cried. It hurt so damn bad because that was what I was being reduced to, was a piece of meat and not a human being with kids. That $35 dollars helped enough that my kids could eat for the week and I got gas to get them back and forth to school. I drank water for the next two weeks, no food."

"Wow! I would have never thought that you were having such a rough time out here."

"Yes, because I really never talk about what's going on with me, it's my business, but I really do need help now."

"No problem, I do understand, I have quite a few good clients, regulars that I can pass to you, so that you will have some steady income coming in. Don't worry I will pass on your number and let them know that you will be taking over from here on out."

"Really Paul? For real? Ohh My God that would help me out soo much! Thank you!"

"Yeah no problem, I don't think that what I have going on with these clients downtown will be your cup of tea."

"Why would you say that?"

"Trust me, ok."

"Well ok, I will take your word for it."

"Hey, one of my clients told me that I should do something with my writing," I confided to Megan.

"Ohh yeah? Like what?'

"My bad, I didn't tell you or you prolly don't know that I actually write short stories and poems in my spare time, Brenda has read some of my work and she thinks it's pretty good."

"That's new news to me; she never told me that you were a writer."

"Well not officially, I just write a little here and there you know."

"I hear ya, and no, I don't know. Let me hear something that you wrote. So you are a poet, hmm? I never thought of you as a man with more than a couple words, but now you write. Interesting."

"Yes, its real good. Janet said that it took her to another place and could not look at me the same since she read about four of my books."

"Four Books?! Wait! What you have four books written?"

"Yeah, but not published, I generally just write about what's in my imagination and it deals with a lot of suppressed sexual tension."

"Blah haaaaaa! What!? Suppressed sexual tension!"

"That's what Janet said."

"Who is Janet? You are speaking about her like I'm supposed to know who she is lol."

"Ohh, you will get to know who she is; that is one of my regular clients. Well, now your regular client. She is a very nice lady and one of my biggest supporters; you'll love her."

"Ok if you say so. Now what is it that you write that is making Janet look at you in some type of way? I need to know, and please read me something."

"I really just go into myself and think of subject matter that has been tucked deep inside and away from my conscious mind."

"Blah blah blah blah! Man just get to what the hell you have written! Wow, you can fuck up a wet dream! Give me some of what you are writing; from the sound of it, sounds real steamy! Ahh you gotta watch the silent smart ones! "

"Ok let me find something real quick. This one is brand new; I wrote this just about a week ago:

'Can I come lay down behind you?

Holding your waist as I kiss on your neck, embracing you as our naked bodies' rock back and forth.

My hand goes from your hip to your breast, caressing your nipples,

With slow strokes you feel me inside you

Deeper I go as we slow grind into pleasure unparalleled, as your body shakes and my dick hardens, ready to unload my cum, my nuts swell and your nipples harden in anticipation of that great release over and over again.

We keep the pace slow so no pain or tiredness just pure pleasure as I hear your body telling me just what it wants

Laying you on your stomach, my hot wet tongue finds places that you never experienced as it presses and licks each and every part of your lap finding your clit.

My mouth engulfs it and my love, dripping tongue glides down your pussy squashing my wetness with your juices

Darting my tongue in your vaginal walls as my hands grips your ass, pulling you closer as my face is buried in your pussy.

Throwing your legs back, ass up, my tongue makes its way further, wetting your ass hole and I insert one solitary finger that slowly disappears as you moan with pleasure as with each stroke my finger and tongue takes you over the edge."

"Ohh damn! Uhh, Paul...you wrote that?"

I could hear her breathing hard on the other end of the phone and she just kept quiet.

"Yes, I wrote every word. Hello? You there?"

"Yes I'm here Paul, it's just that its soo...nasty! Boy! You are a stone cold freak! I never knew you had this in you! Damn your imagination is real... Shit, I can't even get the right words to say after that! Whew! Now I can understand just what the hell Janet is talking about! Cause, ahhh, I need that in my life! Make me wanna see what you working with. Like damn, Paul!"

"I take it that you like it huh?"

"Like it? Really Paul? Like it? You know what they hell you doing trying to be slick and shit! You know what you are doing! And look at me I don't even curse and look, you got me cursing!"

We both laughed. I hadn't really given it much thought, but now hearing the reaction from Megan really made me think that I was really onto something. I was always the type of person that paid attention to detail, which in a sense made me a very good massage therapist, not only taking notes but being capable to translate them into a decent routine for my clients. Janet, well I thought she was just patronizing me because I gave such good massages and she was my client and friend and wouldn't really tell me if I was bad or not. The reaction that Megan gave me really made me think about really going into really writing more.

Hot Stones

"Hands set a blaze, the friction of skin to skin contact has erupted volcanic erotic cosmic waves...from your body to mine."

It seemed like I was now becoming the go-to guy when my ex-classmates needed work, or John needed to use my expertise to woo another client. I had become quite a commodity. I wasn't fully understanding where I fit into this new world that I was thrust into but I made the best out of it. With my classmates taking over my responsibilities with the company, and even my regular clients, I worked out a percentage with them all for the work they were performing, which gave me a much needed break.

I had taken a break from everything and took some time to myself and started to expand my writing portfolio. I really enjoyed writing. I had found my creative zone and it was working out well for me, until I got that fateful call.

Shelly called my out of the blue one day. I hadn't spoken with her since I had taken my hiatus; she left two messages. I retrieved the voice messages.

"Paul, you should know who this is, its Shelly. I was just calling to check up on you. John said that you were taking a break and that your crew of masseurs was really getting the job done. I need to speak to you. I know that we kind of met on some terms that you were not ok with, and is having sex, and you knowing exactly how the company works... Well I mean the way that they operate and all. I know that's not your cup of tea, but I just need to talk to you. Can you please give me a call back when you get this message?"

I listened to the message twice, really paying attention to what she was really trying to say.

Sounded like she really needed to talk to me about something, which made my mind race and wonder just what she had to speak to me about that was so urgent. First thing that came to mind was that somehow she was pregnant or had a disease or something. I sat looking at the phone and trying to get up the nerve to call her back. Just before I picked up to call, the phone started to ring.

"Hello Paul? It's me Shelly..."

"Hey! How are you doing Shelly? I hope everything is good with you and you have good news rather than bad news."

"Huh? What in the world are you rambling about? I just want to see you. Can you meet me at the mall, near the ice cream shop?

"Ohh ok...yeah I will. Ah, when?"

"Right now."

"Oh ok, give me 10 minutes and I will see you there."

She hung up the phone before I was even able to finish my thought. This really had me on edge because it seemed like she was upset about something, and she just hung up.

I arrived at the mall and entered the side door of the food court, making my way over to the ice cream shop. I ordered two concretes, a large cheesecake with honey roasted peanut topping. I found me a seat and waited for her to show up. I spotted her walking down the escalator in the distance; her body was heavenly just like I remembered it. She had a unique walk to her that I studied from the first time we met. Seeing her walk away I copied and pasted her stroll in my mind, permanently branded in my brain. With perfect posture she walked towards me, crossing gently, left leg over right, full firm hips being hugged by her spandex workout pants. Her presence took me back to our lustful night. She came closer to me, waving her hands at me but I did not even blink. I was still in a daze, thinking about our encounter.

"Hello, hello, hello...Paul!"

I jumped at the sound of her voice.

"Yeah!"

"Are you ok?"

"Yes, I'm good, just daydreaming a little."

"Ok, well snap out of it! I see you have my favorite. She eased her way into her chair, grabbed the concrete, inserted a straw and spoon into it and began eating the toppings.

We just stared at one another as we sat and enjoyed our concrete in silence, pausing a few moments at a time with glances and nervous laughter.

"Ok you have my stomach all twisted up; I need to know the purpose of this meeting. I have just about stopped working for the company all together; my friends are actually taking over both the weekly massages and the extra massages for the new clients. What did you want to talk about?"

"Well, if you wanna know, I really feel like we made a connection and I haven't stopped thinking about what happened between us. You made an impression on me that I just can't seem to shake; I really like you...Wait, before you say anything, I don't normally do this, well as far as falling for someone that I just had sex with, but I feel that we have a deeper connection than that. You spent time with me the first time you came over and gave me a massage. You listened to me as I poured out my heart to you. I paid attention to just how you touched me, the way you looked at me; it made me feel...special."

I was floored. I was not ready to hear this from her. I figured it would be some type of bombshell that she was going to drop, but not that she was in love with me. I sat there taking it all in because this really was outta left field. I mean I had crossed the line, true enough, having sex with one of my clients and even getting personal with her, but damn, it felt like it was way more to this than just the sex. I had to really think about what my next words would be because I did feel something between us but I was not trying to get sucked in to whatever she was trying to sell me.

"Ok, let me get this...so you're not pregnant? Have a disease?"

"Huh?! What the hell are you talking about? Damn, you are really a jerk!"

"No, no, no, sorry! I just thought that you were calling to meet me because either you had something along those lines to tell me. Remember, I never mixed business and pleasure. I just chalked up what we did as part of how you -- how they -- handle your business and there was nothing else to it. I mean, you guys live such a wild life and I really am not too comfortable with it."

"To be honest, that was my very first time at one of those parties. I was given something in my drink and it had me feeling like stripping out of my clothes. I was drugged. I think about it being worse. I could have been ganged raped by any of them and would not have had any control over anything. So I wanted to thank you for being there; what we did was partly from a need. I needed it. I was lonely and hadn't been with anyone in a while; I know that it was very risky and irresponsible of me."

"Wow! I didn't know that. Well, I thought you were a pro at this and that's how you got down; really and truly, we don't really know each other so..."

"I'm so sorry. I just got caught up with everything and I have actually quit working for the firm, effective last week. I just wanted to reach out to you and let you know that I was sorry. I know that you follow strict rules of conduct to never mix business with pleasure, I get that. I am a lawyer and should have known better than to put myself in that situation and I deeply apologize for that mistake."

Just then I noticed Tish coming across the food court. Tish was one of the best massage therapists in our class; she really knew what she was doing. I remember getting my very first massage from her; she had a wealth of knowledge about the body and great hands and power for a petite woman. We nicknamed her "Wonder Woman." We all wondered just where the hell did she get all that power out of that little body of hers. She was originally from Kansas but made Atlanta her home right out of high school. She called Atlanta "The Home of The Free," where she could be herself and not have to worry about what others said about her. She's a lesbian, or actually she is bi-, she likes both women and men. You could never really tell what she was on any particular day; some days she would holla at the women who would be at the bar next door to our school during our breaks at night from class, or approach men and get their numbers. She held court with all the crazy stories she would tell us of her wild weekends. She was funny and always kept us laughing.

We made eye contact and her face lit up as she hurried up over to our table. She paused as she got closer and with a confused look on her face she grabbed a chair and sat next to Shelly.

"Hey Boo. How are you?"

"What's up Tish I'm good. And yourself?"

With hearing her voice, Shelly's expression changed, almost like she saw a ghost. She looked up from her concrete, with a spoonful of cheese cake chunks and ice cream in her mouth, and stared into Tish's face.

"Nah, Paulie, I wasn't talking to you. I was talking to this one here. And what's this? Ya'll know each other?"

Fear jumped up into Shelly's face. By the looks of it, Tish and Shelly knew each other quite well. I was the odd man out on this one and I could feel the tension in the air.

"Ohh yes, we know each other...and you know," Shelly started..."

"Yes, I know Shelly real well. She is my ex-girlfriend; well, let's just say most recent ex-girlfriend; she dumped me a week ago!"

Ahh damn! What have I gotten myself into? Someone told me a long time ago that this is a small world and Atlanta was just that, a small world, and anything is possible. With a long pause I watched both Tish's and Shelly's facial expressions change. I needed to get some answers.

"So let me get this straight! You and you are, were, lovers, together? A week ago? How long were you together?"

"Yes!" they both said in unison.

"So again, what is going on with you two?" Tish asked, with her arms crossed and waiting on either one of us to answer.

"Well he is a friend of mine." Shelly said nervously.

"Yes, we all are friends."

Still not knowing how to play this I sat back and kept my mouth shut, just starting to eat the rest of my concrete. As I finished, I just noticed both of them just staring at one another.

"Well, I know Tish from massage school; yeah we went to massage school together."

Tish looked at me as if she wanted me not to say another damn word. She was pissed and wanted to get to the bottom of this. Her face said it all,

"Why the hell is my ex sitting here with him and on what it seems to be a date?"

She took the words right out of my mouth.

"Why the hell are you both sitting here together? Is this a date? What the fuck man? Really? Really? How the fuck this shit happen? Really Shelly? So you left me for him? For him?!"

At that point I just wanted to get Shelly's reaction to all of this. Wow, she was actually in a relationship with Tish the whole time. That would explain the massage table that she had in her home when we first met.

"Wait a minute! So..."

They both put up a finger to let me know to keep my mouth shut, while they ironed out their issue.

"So this explains a lot man, this really explains a lot. The, 'I'm working late,' 'baby I'm tired,' bullshit you was giving me was because you was really stepping out on me with Paulie!? Damn Paul you got it like that for real?"

"No baby, it's not like that, let me explain," Shelly reached for Tish but she pulled her arm away.

Now Tish is a very beautiful woman, not the butch looking lesbian, but what she called "Fem," a girlie girl who loves girls and in her in spare time she chases men also. Shelly, I guess now, is also a "Fem" and now I am caught up in a love triangle with the both of them.

"Well what happened? Why did you break up with her?"

"You happened Paul! I fell for you. The guy that I was talking about was actually Tish. We were going through some things. I lost trust in her and thought that she was out here cheating on me."

"Baby! What!? So you slept with Paulie because you thought that I was out here cheating on you? Really? Look baby look I would never do that to you. I love you soo much, it's just that work has been keeping me busy and you should understand because you are always gone!"

"I just didn't sleep with him it wasn't like that. I went to an office party when you went out of town to do your art show. I was drugged and we had sex."

"What the fuck!? Paulie you slipped my girl a ruffie? For real? You dirty ass motherfucker!"

"No I ain't do that at all! Somebody at the party did, and I was just there. I had recognized her from when we met and I had given her a massage at her house, but nothing happened then. I guess she was drugged and I was drunk and that's when I saw her and we went into another room and it all happened."

"I had no control over myself, I was drugged!"

"Yeah ok and I am supposed to believe that!"

"It's the truth."

"Damn! This shit is all fucked up! This must be the coming out clean day huh? Wow I never thought that this would happen, never in my wildest dreams. My girl would cheat on me with my secret crush."

Now that was a fucking bombshell! I had no idea that Tish had something for me. She was cute and all, and yeah, I really was feeling her, but we just never crossed that line. Shelly and I were both shocked and we stared at one another in silence.

"Yes! Yes! Yes! I said it! I had a thing for you when we were in school. We never really had time to really talk about it but I did have a thing for you. I thought you were corny as fuck and a lame but you were real cute. You wasn't real rough around the edges, very intelligent and confident. You knew your shit; that's what was soo attractive about you. Plus, you just a real nice guy but I never really got to know you like that. And those hands of yours! Fuck! I knew she would have eventually slept with you. The way you touch a woman, there is no way in this world that she wouldn't get aroused."

There was an awkward silence; I had to process all of what just went down.

"Well I am so sorry for doing this to you...I just thought…"

"Yes I know baby, but it's kind of fucked up how you just quit on me and not really tell me why."

"Paul wasn't the reason why I broke up with you totally; it was just that we stopped spending time together and I got lonely. I wanted more and my insecurities got the best of me. Do you forgive me?"

"Yes I forgive you baby. I still love you."

"Ok hold up! I hate to break up this Doctor Phil moment! But I feel bad that this happened also. I am sorry that I was blessed with the best pair of hands on earth."

"Shut up Paul!"

"Well the good news is that she quit her job so now you both will have time to spend with each other."

"What? You quit your job? Why?"

"It's a long story but I will tell you in detail later."

"I feel bad about this whole thing; please allow me to take you both to dinner Friday. Will that be ok?"

"Yes that would be fine so we can discuss a little bit further where we go from here."

Tish had a devilish look on her face. I have seen this look before. I knew she had something up her sleeve. We all left and went our separate ways and it was a date! I would be on a date with two beautiful women Friday and I was dying of anticipation of what would come next.

Tantric

"Awakening what's asleep inside of you. Pleasuring you back to sleep."

The business picked up and I was seeing my return from my new employees growing. "Employees," yes that sounded so nice. I had my classmates working for me and taking over the contract and even my own personal clients. I was just sitting back and collecting my percentages. From the looks of it, there were no complaints at all; seemed like everyone was happy with their jobs.

My last talk with John he wanted me to have two to three of my classmates meet a new client of theirs and it really involved some sexual pleasures. This was really getting outta hand but I didn't want to mess up the money train, so I called around to get the second person who may want to involve themselves with this tall order. I knew that Daniel was already on board. I called around to see who would be the number two on this job but no takers, so I was reluctantly pulled back into the freak show.

"My dude! I just got the call from John and he told me about this crazy ass party and new clients that he wants us to go to tonight! You down?"

"Hey Daniel, well yeah, I guess we got to go get this money huh?"

"Damn right my dude! Get this money! Fuck some bitches and party!"

"Don't know about the 'fucking bitches' part but I am ready to party and get this money."

"Hahhaahah! Ol' Paulie about to shake a tail feather get your dick wet and get you some regular cunt!"

"Hey, I know that John alluded to doing more than a massage but I am going to keep it professional and do my job."

"Yeah, 'do your job' as professional as you can do it and I'm sure they gonna love it my dude!"

Daniel dropped the phone and I could hear him in the background laughing his head off. I hung up and read the rest of the instructions that John had in the email.

John left a long email about what we were to go pickup for the party, which involved liquor and beer that was already ready at the local AJ Package store. I swung by and the guy came out with a dolly full to the top with boxes. I opened the back of my truck and we loaded all of the items.

This was really out of the scope of work that I normally perform and against all of my rules of professionalism but they were paying top dollar and I wasn't about to turn this job down. Daniel went ahead of me to set up the tables. I had never been to this location before, off Northside Drive; the parking lot wasn't well lit and my gps guided me all the way to the rear entrance. I called up to Daniel to come help me get the beer and liquor upstairs.

"My Dude! What's poppin? We here jive early so I have everything already setup in the VIP area. It looks like John took over this place because all you see is banners everywhere with the company's name on it. Must be some big time clients he trying to woo. And the sound system is off the muthafuckin chain my dude! They said that doors don't open till 8:30 tonight and our folks will be ready around 8:45 sharp."

We had everything ready for the guests and all the free beer and liquor they could drink, I spoke with the bartenders and they assured me they would take over from there. I stepped out of the VIP area to get some air and check the place out. By 8:25 pm a long line had formed outside and the music was blaring. I took a couple shots of Patron and mixed it with beer and a couple shots of Remy Red and Jack.

Daniel told me to try and take the edge off and drink a little more and by 8:45 I was literally seeing double, I hadn't eaten anything all day so the alcohol rushed right to my head. The open bar was full of food so I just helped myself to whatever was close to fill my stomach. I had done it, full and drunk, not a good combination for a non-drinker, plus having to work that night, would certainly be a recipe for disaster.

Our clients were late and we had no idea just who we were supposed to be rendering services for out of the crowded club. There was a mixture of people just about all ages, men and women, and they were having a good time. I saw no one sitting down; the dance floor was packed. I could hear the DJ in the distance yelling something over the mic. I could not make out what it was but it got the crowd hyped. They started jumping up and down and the place really went crazy. Daniel was over in the corner with his third plate of food and a wine bottle he was drinking directly from and I could hear him complaining about 'the bitches.'

"Man I'm waiting for these bitches to come on, stop fucking dancing and come let my hands rub all over their sweaty bodies."

Well if you ask me, I would rather them not be sweaty but Daniel could care less. He was all about getting 'the bitches,' making them wet so that he could get his dick wet.

He complained like that for about another hour, and still no signs of our clients, or 'the bitches,' so we just waited. It really didn't bother me any because we had four more hours to go and then we would be done.

Finally, the club promoter came into the VIP section and introduced himself to us, I could just about hear every other word he spoke, the music was blaring and the alcohol had me close to passing out. He instructed the guests behind him to come into the VIP room. They filed into the room, and as they walked in, I made a mental note, counting them as they sat down. One of them walked over and laid down on one of the tables pointing to his back.

Both Daniel and I looked at each other as to say, "Not Me!" I was not going to massage a man, especially not dressed like that. This was something that took both of us by surprise to say the least. He had on some daisy duke booty shorts that left very little to imagination, a Marilyn Monroe printed shirt, and with purple loafers and a pair of the hairiest legs I had ever seen.

Daniel pulled me to him then yelled in my ear,

"My Dude, you got this one! I ain't even fucking with this. I will give you all of my half of money for this job. I will wait for a bitch to come to my table, but you got The Long Ranger!"

I tried yelling back to let him know that I was refusing the job also but he backed away and then shoved me in the back towards the table. The guy stood back up and came close to me and yelled in my ear.

"Don't be scared! I won't bite...that hard!" He dropped back on the table laughing hysterically.

I guess he could tell that this was not my type of party and him and his friends started chanting drunk, crazy and rowdy,

"Dooo it! Dooo it!"

I attempted compressions on his shoulders, trying to avoid skin to skin contact, as his crop-cut shirt kept inching up closer to his shoulders. He didn't help the situation with his squirming and laughing while I massaged his back. Daniel stood over in the corner making eye contact with me and nodding his head, as to say come over to him. I finished the back massage and the guy jumped up from the table, handing me a card and a twenty dollar bill. He raised his hands up and closed his eyes doing a shimmy and smacked me on the ass as he ran over to the other side of the room and started dancing seductively in the corner staring and laughing at me. Once I got over to Daniel, he had this real weird and disgusted look on his face.

"What?!" I yelled at him as he motioned for me to come closer to him.

"My dude we up in crispy crème, butt kake heaven, T Bag Central, Pirates of the Caribbean, Land of the lost brown eye chasers! Shit Chasers! We in a Gay Club man!!!!"

I got the last part that he was yelling. I looked around as he was saying it. Right there and right then, it dawned on me. We were in an all-male guy club and our clients were majority gay men. I was a little unnerved because I had never been in a gay club. I looked around and it all became clearer; the men were grinding on each other while others had conversations over in the corner where they were so close they were almost sitting in each other's laps. I saw a couple kissing and dancing as one of them grabbed and groped the other man's ass. I felt a tap on my shoulder and it was another man who wanted a massage. And this time he started to take off all of his clothes and go on the table laying there fully bare, holding a hand over his penis. That was my cue to get lost!

I walked out of the VIP and Daniel was hot on my heels, yelling and cursing as I headed towards the manager's office. We stopped in a long line headed towards the restrooms and I saw a familiar face. It was

Chase. He was standing by the bathroom waiting to get in; I ran up to him and grabbed his arm.

"Chase!"

"Paulie? Paulie what the hell you doing out here? Ahh shit and Daniel to? Ya'll want to tell me something?"

"Nah my dude, it ain't nothing like that, not that type of party!"

"Well you can surely fool me because if you look around...Ah bae-bae! It is that type of party!"

"I know Chase and I need a big favor of you right now, I didn't know that it was this type of party at all and I want out! I will pay you for taking over. Can you please help out?"

"Yeah My Dude, I will double that! Here's my cut for you," Daniel said, reaching into his pocket and passing the wad of money over to Chase.

"Well damn! How much is this?"

"That's a G my dude!"

"Well alright now! Give me body bae-bae! I will take this paper and take over! So everything is already setup upstairs?"

"Yes everything is already setup and ready to go."

Chase grabbed my arm and we walked over to the other side of the club and into a small room away from the noise.

"Look Paulie, I want to thank you for all that you have done for me and believe me, it has been way more money than I have had since I started doing my thing. But you and Danny boy better get your shit together."

"Huh? I'm lost?"

"Yes bae-bae! Money is green and I'm not complaining that you are passing it on to me, but just think what we do for a living. Yes it can get a little racy but that's up to you where you take it or not, but you passing up a lot of money being closed minded."

"Well thank you Chase but I'm not there yet, I can't see myself massaging a man who is fully naked holding his dick!"

"Wow!! Where at, hunti, please let me know where he is! Lol. Hey I'm just messing with you, and I do understand how you feel. I'm sorry John did not give you a heads up. But I got it from here, I know the club owner so you can come pick up your tables and gear in the morning."

"Thank you Chase I really appreciate it." Hugging him I turned and started to walk away.

"Ahh no you didn't! Excuse me, hunti!" Clapping his hands and rolling his neck with his hand out. "I need my money child!"

Walking back over to him I emptied my pockets and gave him my portion.

"Thank you, Paulie, I will give you back your percentages tomorrow. Cool?"

I nodded my head in agreement.

I walked outside looking for Daniel and he texted to meet him around back where our cars were parked.

"My dude, I swear I'ma kill your boy John! On everything he fucking set us up like shit!"

"Well I guess we should have asked about the job before we took it."

We both stopped and looked at each other and busted out laughing.

"Your boy wanted you to rub him down and grab his ass! He was ready butt ball naked just holding his dick giving you those eyes!"

"Man don't remind me! I'm just glad I'm out of there! That was real crazy and I was not ready for something like that!"

"Not you 'Mr. Manipulation of Soft Tissue' you should have been fine with it right? Its only muscle and tissue remember?"

"Naw this was way more than that; that dude was tryna get me!"

We laughed a little more and spoke about just how many men up in there didn't even look like they were gay at all. Some of them looked like the type that would knock you out just looking at them wrong. The range of age from young and old and all nationalities really made us think about the dynamic and sheer number of gay men in one area. But then again, I had to remember just where we were, in Atlanta.

The night was still young so Daniel suggested that we go to the strip club to get our minds right.

"Man, I need to look at some naked women to get my mind clear from all the shit that I just saw."

"No doubt! I feel you! Magic City it is!"

We made up for the crazy start of our weekend; tipping strippers grabbing ass and getting totally wasted, Daniel almost got kicked out of the club twice.

Later on that morning I woke up with the worst hangover I ever had in my life, my first hangover! The majority of the rest of the morning was a complete blur. Daniel had me popping pills and sipping on sizzurp, whatever that was, it had me having an out-of-body experience. I got out of bed and walked to the bathroom only to find that apparently we had brought the strip club home with us, I saw four naked bodies sprawled all over the couch, floor and even another two at the head of my bed. Daniel was nowhere in sight. I looked around my house and could not find him anywhere. But he left a note:

"My dude...had to bounce. Going shopping wit my bitch, holla at you lata!"

I took a shower and could smell the aroma of eggs, bacon and fried potatoes coming from the kitchen. The girls were up and two of them were in the kitchen making breakfast while the rest were cleaning up my house. Apparently, we had booked the strippers for a private party back at my place and they had signed a contract that Daniel had drawn up and they were now my new clients.

I had at least two previous clients that were strippers and our business relationships ended quickly when they thought they could trade services for serving me. That was the old me; I had never thought to mix business and pleasure before, because it was risky and it just didn't mix for me. I couldn't believe my eyes that I had six beautiful women in my house, cooking and cleaning; I had died and gone to heaven, stripper heaven at that.

I reintroduced myself to all of the girls. Daniel had told them all that I was harmless and even gay and not interested in women at all. That gained their trust I guess; hell they ate it up because before long they were asking about fashion and how to apply their makeup correctly. I excused myself and jumped on the phone calling Daniel.

"What's up, my dude?" Daniel yelled in the phone as he picked up on the other line.

"Shit! You tell me! I guess you told all the strippers that I was gay and harmless? What's up with that?"

"Wait, wait, wait my nigga! Check this out ok; I did you a favor and shit, now you gonna get buck wit me?"

"Slow down man! I was just asking you a question!"

"Nah, but peep this my dude, you can get mad cheddar now fucking wit the stripper bitches if they think you ain't gonna try shit wit them, ya dig? So you know I'm always on the grind, so when we was out last night I figured I'd holla at these hoes for you and hook that shit up for you. Now you got that shit on lock, cause these bitches always need a nigga to rub they feet and lower back and shit! You know them hoes bodies be hurting like shit!"

Daniel had said enough "hoes" and "bitches" for my liking and I had to set him straight.

"Look Daniel, these are women that you are talking about who just so happen to dance and entertain assholes like you and I, at times, but that's not my point. They deserve respect to so watch what the hell comes out of your mouth when you speak about these women; you have no idea why they took up this job as a profession. Shit you lack morals right along with how you feel about them. Hell your MO has always been about "getting the bitches, some ass and some wet-wet." You're worse off than them!"

Right then he cuts me off,

"Well damn dude, I ain't mean to get you upset; super save a hoe ass nigga! I was just trying to do you a fucking favor!"

"Nah, I appreciate the gesture, but you going to have to ease up."

"Ok, I got you my dude, so go ahead and make that dough and yeah, I will kind of calm that shit down. You owe me like shit though! Fuck you square ass nigga I'm out!"

Hell, it never fails. Daniel is crazy, but gotta love him because he is all about his money and has shown to be a good asset for business. I ate breakfast and we all exchanged information and which days they would come through for service.

I got a call from Tish later, after all the girls left. She wanted to set up a meeting with everyone at my house later on that night, just to all catch up. I made the calls to everyone and made plans for later that night. I couldn't wait to get all my ex classmates together again, they had been actually working for me indirectly for a couple of months now with the contract and were doing quite well and even earned a new contract with another company in the Castleberry Hills area.

I wanted to throw a party for a change and surprise my friends. They always teased me for being too uptight and a square, so I made a few calls and put my plan into action. I called Daniel and told him the get together started at 8:30 and told the rest of them to be here by 7. With Daniel, anything goes, so I wanted to get some breathing room before his crazy ass stepped in the door again. The first ones to arrive were Tish and Megan, arriving promptly at 7pm. I greeted both of them at the front door.

"Hello Ladies, come on in and make yourself at home."

Megan smiled at me and kissed me on the cheek while Tish just eyeballed me and sat down on my couch grabbing the remote to watch T.V.

"Hey what's on T.V? "Tish demanded. Visibly annoyed with her, Megan responded,

"Tish! You are so damn rude! You didn't even give the man a hug or even speak to him when we came in. What is your problem?"

"I don't have a problem Megan, but Paul has a problem," Tish fired back while rolling her eyes.

"Wait a minute! Tish this was your idea for all of us to meet up here at my house and now you come in with an attitude! Why?"

"Well Megan! If you really want to know what's going on, I will tell you." Tish turned towards Megan, but grinned at me, "Paulie here has been sleeping with my girlfriend!"

"Wait? What?! You have to be kidding me? Did he know that she was your girlfriend? I need to know details! Tell me!"

Megan ran over to the couch and jumped right next to Tish, excitedly waiting to hear the juice.

"Come on Tish! I thought we already went over this," I pleaded with her.

Tish just rolled her eyes, pulled Megan in real close and started to whisper in her ear about what happened between me and Shelly. I'd had enough, so I just excused myself from the room while they acted like teenage gossip girls. By the time I entered the living room again, the whole bunch was there, Daniel, Chase, Megan, and Tish, all sitting on my couch.

"Hey what's going on guys," I asked nervously, feeling like I was the topic of conversation.

"Paulie!" I hear from the group in unison.

"Damn, my dude, you are a straight savage! Knocking off carpet munchers and turning them straight!"

"Shut the hell up Daniel!"

"Fuck you asshole," Tish fired back at him, throwing her drink in his face.

"Wait! Wait! Wait! Please don't start that shit. Daniel you don't ever know what to say out your mouth! Tish, never mind his crazy ass; he ain't right."

Megan jumped in grabbing Tish's arm and leading her to the kitchen.

"Daniel, Daniel, Daniel, you are so damn messy! Ion really give a damn about what you say! Huh, hunti! I know I'm fab so your words don't matter! Damn you really got to her cause ahh, hunti is a bitch! Huh child...Tish you really need to stop fucking wit community pussy! I told you before and this ain't even the first time!"

Chase sat back on the couch with his legs crossed and sipped on his mixed drink.

"Shut the fuck up, Chase, I know what the hell you told me before but it ain't got shit to do with what's coming outta that asshole's mouth! Now do it?"

Chase didn't respond, he lightly grinned and swung his legs as he continued to drink.

Tish, Megan, and Daniel got into a shouting match where each one of them tried to convince the other one who was wrong. Chase just sat there mesmerized.

"Paulie! Thank you, child. This shit right here has made my fucking week! No! No! No! Bitch, you started it, now finish it!"

Chase jumped off the couch and pushed Daniel in his back, egging him on to keep up the fighting.

"Heeeey!! Ok now I ain't want this shit to go on! I need for everybody to just calm the fuck down!" I yelled at the top of my lungs. Everybody stopped what they were doing and just stared at me.

"Uuuuhhhwee! This nigga done grew some balls!" Daniel yelled out.

"Wait for once in your life! Stop calling everyone "Nigga! You call white people, Chinese people, Spanish people, black people that word! Hell! I bet you call your doctor, your mailman your dog..," Daniel interrupted me.

"Yeah! My nigga!"

Everyone started laughing. By some strange reasoning, Daniel' ignorant antics lightened up the mood and everyone calmed down.

"Ok my dude I will take that into consideration, and I would like to also apologize to all of you for how I spoke earlier. You know it's hard to break a habit that has been part of my life ever since I was 9 years old. But I will do better. Tish I am soo sorry for calling you a carpet muncher; we love the same thing and believe me pussy don't taste like no carpet."

"Somebody kill this fucker already! I mean damn! You can't be serious for one fucking second. Can you?" Tish hits Daniel in his chest.

"Ok, this is real. Yes I am sorry. Can you accept my apology?"

"Yes I accept it." Tish reached out to Daniel and they embraced.

Everyone clapped.

"Good God! I am soo happy that ya'll done stopped with all this drama! Hell why be upset over spoiled milk and community pussy?" Chase countered, and sat back in pure delight, sipping his drink.

"If you wanna know why I am upset Chase, is because I really loved her and she did the unthinkable just recently." Tish looks at me and rolls her eyes.

"Mmmm go right ahead baby and spill the T-E-A!"

"She slept with Paulie while we were on a break."

Chase rolls off the couch and on to the floor, throwing his drink all over my leather couch; he rolls then jumps up and runs out the living room into the kitchen. He comes back in, screaming and circling the group, as we watch him, flapping his arms and waving a cloth around.

"Shut the front door! Euhhwee not this one?"

As he points his finger at me and dances around me. "Girrlah!! That's what all this hoopalah is all about! This Paulie's coming clean party and I'm late as usual! Paulie got that fire bae bae! Hunti! He turned a crooked one straight! I'm finna faint... Ima faint, girl... this is too much!"

Chase spins around and drops down on the couch still laughing to himself.

"Well, damn, Tish, I don't know why you so damn mad at the dude. You did say you and your old lady was on a break so anything goes," Daniel yells while trying to give me a hi-five. I left him hanging.

"Naw, Daniel it's not like that, but I still felt like she cheated on me and especially once I found out with who, but that ain't even it either."

Tish pauses and everyone just waits to see what else she has to say. Then she leaves out of the room and comes back with a black bag.

"Ohh, shit, she got a gun!!" Daniel yells, then rushes the other way into the kitchen.

Chase screams, Megan covers her face with a pillow, as Tish stands there and digs into her bag. I flinch and plead with her,

"Now Tish, come on! I didn't even know that she had anyone else, or you know...ahh with you."

Tish turns and looks at me and smiles, "You dumb ass! I don't have a gun!" She pulls out a black book.

"Hey! Is that my book?" I yelled at her, wondering how in the world did she get it.

"Yes, this is your book, Freaky Boy! Janet gave it to me, she liked your writing so much the last time that you gave her a massage she stole it from you."

"Ole child, I thought it was gonna be 'Murder She Wrote' or an episode of 'Snapped' up in this place. You went for that bag and I messed up my pad messin wit you!"

Chase adjusted his crouch and began to laugh again.

"Boi, stop! You know you can't wear no damn pad with that flap!"

At that, both Tish and Chase fell to the couch laughing.

"Yeah, Paulie is a straight freak! He damn sure showed my ex-girl some new moves, enough to make her go straight forsho!"

"Bitch, Where!?" Chase screamed. "Really? Are you being for real Tish? So what the hell is he writing up in this damn book?"

Tish hands Chase the book and they sit back on the couch.

"Well, your secret is out now...better embrace it this time," Megan says, looking at me and smiling.

"My dude, I'm lost like shit! What type of shit is going on in that book they reading?"

"It's a book that I wrote about a year ago and it just have a lot of fantasy and stories in it"

Tish interrupts me,

"Fucking liar! It has more that some little fantasy and stories in it! Daniel let's call it XXX and he is the fucking director and leading man in this scripted porn movie!"

"Ahh shit, homie! You getting down like that?! They always say watch out for the quiet ones! Damn! They into that shit! Hey let me read something," Daniel demands and jumps on the couch.

"Dayumn! I think I'm wet! So damn descriptive...hmmm. Ohh wow...Girlah! You gonna make me lose my virginity, Paulie."

"Shidd! It's been gone a long time ago boy!" Daniel fires back.

Everyone starts laughing as they keep reading my book, page by page. Just then my cell phone rings and I excuse myself from the room.

"Hello?"

"Hey, Paul. How are you doing?" It was Shelly.

"What's going on with you Shelly? I got all of the gang here now, and yes, Tish just blew up at me over what happened between us."

"Damn, well we did have a blowout also the day that we all met at the mall, and that's kind of the reason that I called you. I expressed to her that I had an interest in exploring my options, since we were not really working out because of her jealous ways and insecurities. I just couldn't take it anymore and the thing with you and I...well, I told her what made me interested in you and she got real mad at me and cried and stomped out the house. She left this book here and I read it and didn't realize that it was yours and I could really see where your mind is. You really have such a freaky mind and that made me even hotter for you."

"Whoa! Wait! You read my book too?"

"Too?"

"Well, yeah, she brought my book with her and now everyone else is in my living room reading it"

"Ohh, ok. Well it's definitely a great read, not for young eyes for real, very erotic. Question...So that's what made your massages soo intimate? The way you think when you are doing them? Or was it your attraction to me?"

"Hard question to answer right now, being that I am really feeling a little annoyed that my personal business is all out and I feel violated because I did not give her my book."

"Well, I am sorry. I didn't know that you felt this way, but I can understand, because no one wants their personal property stolen and looked at without their permission. I get that, but...it's really good! You would have never guessed that you would write something like that. I know from personal experience with you that those words you have written… day-um they do come to life."

"Well that's another story."

"Can I see you again? I really want to see you again; Tish does not have to know. I am done with her and want to have another night with you."

"Shit! That will not be a good idea, the way that she is going off now! She will kill me and you. No! I'm sorry but that's not happening!" I hung up the phone immediately.

Damn this chick is crazy to think that we can still be messing with each other after I found out that she was Tish's ex-girlfriend. Hell naw, I'm not stupid. I could hear everyone in the living room still arguing about my book. I turned the music up louder to try and drown them out. I had a lot to think about and this was not going how I planned. I wanted to just have a get together and see how everyone was doing but now I am the center of attention.

"Paulie!! Paulie!! Where you go?"

Megan comes running into the kitchen looking for me.

"I'm right here; I just had to take a call. What's going on out here?"

"Well, they are still going over your book, lol. I got to say that it s very good, real juicy and XXX rated. Damn, it's actually better than he first thing you read me that was a teaser; now this one is the whole script. How are you doing?"

"I'm good; I just want to make sure that things have calmed down with Tish before I come back out there."

"Damn, you had sex with her girl though. She gonna still be upset with you."

"I didn't even know that was her girl, I had no idea."

"Yeah, but she is still blaming you for breaking up her relationship. And the book does not help, because she is thinking that one of those stories is about her girlfriend and it's really getting to her."

"I wrote that book two years ago! I didn't even know her girlfriend back then. Well, hopefully we can get to the reason that I wanted all of you to come here, so we could catch up. I wanted to have a few drinks, good food and music and catch up and brainstorm on the new business venture."

"New business venture? Hmm, what do you have up under your sleeve? Are you looking to start a business with us all in partnership with you?"

"I figured, since we all are kind of working together now, we could actually expand, because we now have two good contracts and maybe we can use the clout from the two companies and secure a larger contract, or even a brick and mortar. But we need to have everyone on the same page, you know."

"Yes, I do agree, we all need to be on the same page. That sounds good. Now let's see how you can sell it to everyone."

Megan left the kitchen and headed back to the living room; I poured me a strong drink and downed a couple shots. I knew that I had to try and calm down Tish so that I could have the floor, so we all could come to some type of resolution and talk business.

I watched from the kitchen as Megan walked back to the living room. I hadn't really noticed her until now; she wore a form fitting blue skirt and midsized heels, which showed off her shapely tanned legs. Her full hips and butt shook each time she took a step, swaying back and forth. Her hair fell below her shoulders, dark and curly; the scent of her perfume filled the air and filled my nose as she walked away. She turned and noticed me staring.

"You looking kind of hard aren't you?" she asked with a smile.

"Huh? What? Naw I was thinking about something."

"Yeah, I bet! I wonder which one of your fantasies I just dropped into in your mind. Inquiring minds want to know."

Changing the subject, I just gave her a wink and addressed the elephant in the room.

"Ok! Ok! Ok! I'm sure you all had enough reading for today! Give me my book!"

"Uhh, Hell No! Let's say this is my book now! This is what wet dreams are made of and I haven't had one in a long time, so please Paulie, don't do me like that!" Chase falls to his knees and grabs onto my leg acting like a dog in heat.

"Ewwl! Get off of my leg, dude!"

"You ain't never lied Chase! It is so damn detailed and the mentioning of body parts I didn't even know existed, but better yet, what the hell he can do to those body parts that had me soo damn upset!" Tish takes aim and hits me square between the eyes with the back of the book.

"Damn, you could've taken his eye out Tish!! Damn! You alright my dude? Tish, you may need to let Paulie, sex you over a bit, so you can get out all of that pent-up aggression. You too damn fine to be so damn mean!"

"Fuck you, Daniel!"

"Yes! Please Do! Fuck me, Tish and do me Goooood!"

Tish starts swinging on Daniel and hitting him in the chest. Chase grabs her and sits her down on the couch.

"Child! Sit your ass down, Scary J Blige! We don't want or need any more drama, so take several seats! Paulie, now what the hell are we doing next since this one..," Chase points at Tish and rolls his eyes. "...can't seem to keep her attitude in check and just fucking mad at the world!"

"Well, it's about damn time! I was getting kind of...tired of this drama." Megan shouts out loud, surprising even herself as she tried to take back the words that left her mouth into everyone's ears.

Everyone laughs. Megan is always the quiet one and for her to say something, it must've really gotten on her nerves.

"I'm sorry, ya'll, it just got the best of me and I lost it." Tish responds with her head down.

"Yeah, I'm sure it got the best of you. That Ole Paulie was giving your girl the best that he's got!" Daniel jumps up and starts making humping moves on the other couch armrest.

"Ok, enough is enough! Guys, I want to catch up and talk to you all about something so can we just drop this for now and get back to it later?"

Everyone nods their heads.

"I just want to do a round table discussion about these contracts and actually just going out there on our own and partner up and have a company of our own."

"Hell, Yeah, Home boy! That's what I'm talking about! So we still gonna be into that freak shit with John and them?"

"Well, I see that's your cup of tea, but I was seeing if anyone else wanted to continue with working and owning their own part of the business, Now the "Freak Shit?" That's right up your alley. I don't think that we are gonna leave those contracts at all, just branching out to a larger clientele base, you know."

"Ohh, ok that will work!"

"Now that you mentioned it, Paulie, I was approached by one of the associates at John's firm last week, and you know me, I'm not really into all that shit and happy endings like your boy Daniel is. Actually, I don't do it at all. But he made me feel real uncomfortable and I guess, since word got around that Daniel was "Mr. Pleasure," I guess he thought we're all doing it. He mentioned giving me an extra $100 to have sex with him after I was done with his massage. I rejected him and he got real upset. He was a new client with John and I guess John told him along the lines that I would take care of him and whatever he needed. I was meaning to tell you about it but I decided to just quit. So I haven't been working with them for the last five days."

Megan looked around, noticeably upset about what had happened to her.

"Damn, I am soo sorry Megan, I didn't mean for you to have to go through something like this. I thought that the new clients were different. I guess, when dealing with John, birds of a feather flock together. There are real freaks over there," I told her.

"Hmm, looks who's talking? The biggest freak of them all, Paulie," Tish fires at me and Chase grabs her again, trying to keep her calm.

"What the hell you put in these damn drinks Paulie? Got your girl on edge! Look at her! She is all fucked up now!"

Tish is just staring at me, like if she could shoot beams of fire out of her eyes she would and watch me burn to death.

"Damn, Tish! If looks could kill I would be dead right now!"

She shook her head and flipped the bird at me.

"You know I have kids and I'm not willing to do that to myself, or put them in any type of danger," Megan said, lowering her head.

"Well, I will get to the bottom of it for you, Megan, and make sure that you are well compensated for your time. I know that it can be hard for us out here, where folks have their own agendas. I got your back. Ok?"

I felt real bad about what she was going through.

"Yo Paulie, that's the name of the game and I ain't got no problems serving theses bitches. Cause they lonely and they need that work, so I got that for them! Yeah, Megan, a lot of this ain't for everybody. I know that you got into this field to make a difference, like Paulie did but I am making a difference also. Making them feel gooood!" Daniel falls back on the couch humping the air.

"Damn! Shit ain't change with this asshole! Still fucking young minded! I'm sure your crazy ass is still single and I'm surprised you ain't catching no fucking charge yet!" Tish fires back at Daniel.

"Well, if you must know, Ms. Drama, I am engaged to get married. Yeah, your man has found someone freakier than me! And I would like to thank Paulie for the hook-up, cause I have been the happiest that I have ever been."

"Huh? What are you talking about," Daniel?

"The party that you didn't want to do, the divorcee party? Remember?"

"Ohh, Yeah! I remember the one you came out with all of that money that I thought you robbed them. Lol."

"Well, me and Tasha are getting married in March. And you all are invited!"

"Well congratulations, I think. How the hell did all of that happen?"

"Well, as you know, we hit it off, after I hit her and her girlfriends off, you dig? Yeah, so after that we have been attached at the hip and she even have me do private parties with her and her girlfriends. We have threesomes on the regular with her good friend. Hell, it's gonna be me marrying into her and her girlfriends' life. Lol! I got two freaks!"

"Ohh-M-G! This crazy ass fucker done hit the freak mother load! Well I'm happy for you; now you can stop bothering me for new clients! Keep your shit over there!"Chase responds.

"Ohh, hold up girlfriend! Last time I checked, you was the one who benefited off of me! Short memory, having sweet and low muthafucka! Don't let me tell your little secrets, my dude, while you bullshiting!"

"Uhh, Wait, what? What secrets?"

This reveal got Tish's attention as she jumped up from the couch.

"Well, looks like your boy has been playing on both sides of the tracks lately, and got a sweet little run going, and when I found out, I wanted in, you know, to expand on my bitches. And I found out homeboy is a fucking beast! Got those bitches coming back for more than a massage."

"Ohh, damn! So you having sex with women now Chase? I wanna know how this came about, boo-boo," Megan shouts out.

The room got louder with everyone having their separate conversations and all the while putting Chase on the hot seat, trying to get some information out of him, and the truth.

"Well, I done been with women before...it's not like I been gay all of my life."

"Well, we kinda figured you hadn't been gay all your life, but it had to be a point where you identified and something happened to make you go the other way. Right?"

Chase put his head down and replied, "Yes."

Chase took another shot and went back to start filling his glass up more with wine, when Tish stopped him and grabbed his hand.

"Look, I know how you feel, but I don't know how it happened and when you decided to be gay, but believe me, I know that it has to be a story behind it. Hell, I have a story of my own."

"Yeah, dude, I'm sure we would all like to know about this new revelation and just how did you get the way that you are," Daniel said, walking over to Chase and patting him on the back.

"Hey! Ok, look, I want to first say something," I yelled, assuming control of the floor. "Tish, I would like to apologize again; I didn't know that Shelly was your girl. And I'm seeing that we all have some skeletons in our closets, and we all being friends, I think that we need to respect each other's life and even things that have not gone down the way we thought it should be. Let's forgive and move on. I have big plans for all of us with this new business venture. I need everybody to be on the same page, and furthermore, no surprises. So please speak your mind or be honest about what's going on."

"Thank you, Paulie, and yes, I accept your apology and I am sorry also, being mad with you. I was just hurt," Tish said.

She stands up and gives me a big hug. She rolls up out of the hug and plants a big kiss on me, lips to lips, and even a flick of her tongue graces my top lip.

I don't think that anyone else caught the tongue flick, but I definitely felt it and had a good clue of her intentions. She returned to her seat and just stared at me. I could feel my excitement creeping up on me, as my penis started to stiffen in my pants. I had to switch gears and not think of what just happened.

"Huh, huh, Chase? What's going on? What's this new news all about?" I asked nervously.

"Well damn, I guess I'm not going to get outta here without answering that question, huh?"

"Ohhh!!" Everyone yells.

We are shocked to hear Chase speak a bit normal, without all the "Child! BaeBae! Hunti," and high pitched voice he usually speaks with. His voice was low and deep. He had our attention.

"Like I said, I was not always like this. I was 15 when my life changed forever. Before that, I had had sex with four girls." He nods his head and sucks back the tears.

I will admit, I was a bit feminine when I was coming up. I was in a house full of girls, four older sisters, my mom and grandma, no male insight. I would play with dolls and imitate my sisters and mother at a young age, and they thought it was cute. I had not thought of being gay, I just liked what they liked, in music, shows and even how they made themselves up in the mirror. I guess I was just a product of my environment. I would sit for hours, watching TV and never even thought about going outside to play football or basketball with the boys. And when I did, I was always on the sideline.

The very first time that I ever even thought about another boy or man being attractive to me is when my oldest sister had a crush on this basketball player. He liked her, so he would wind up on our porch just about every day, looking for her, but she was too shy to come outside. He came around one day and she was not there; she was out with her girls. He noticed me looking at him from the window and asked me if it was ok if he could come in and wait for her.

I let him in, but he was not really waiting on her, he was actually there for me. He expressed his interest in me and asked me not to tell anybody about it. I guess he could just sense that I had secretly had a thing for him. I didn't feel that I was gay at that point; I just could feel the overwhelming lust that my sister felt for him, and I too felt that strange way when he looked at me. I knew it was wrong, because a boy is not supposed to like another boy, but he looked and smelled so damn good.

So it happened. It was new, scary and mind blowing, all at the same time. He touched me and I touched him in ways that were so wrong, but felt so damn right. But that didn't last long. He brutally beat me after forcefully having sex with me.

My sister found me in my room, unconscious, bloody and naked. I never really recovered from that day, I started to inflict the pain that I had felt that day on others, I identified with being a homosexual male years later. I had come to grips that I really loved men. After the physical scars had healed, my secret remained with me. My sister never even knew that I had been with her crush, and no one else other than him, and now you guys even knew what happened.

All of my relationships with both women and men all failed, I am super-aggressive and hardheaded, and I call the shots. My therapist said that it was me taking back control of myself, the self that was lost when he...raped me. I tried for years to tell myself that it was consensual and that I wanted it but not that way, I didn't ask to be assaulted and left for dead. I struggled with it and wanted to keep it a secret, but it is tearing my whole life up. I have victimized many lovers because I swore to myself that I would never be a victim again.

That day was the first and the last time that any man had sex with me in that way, I don't get fucked! I fuck them!"

Chase runs into the kitchen and with a loud roar, "Ugggh!" he hits the floor and cries uncontrollably.

Megan rushes in to console him as everyone else sits there in a daze, trying to process all of what we just heard.

"Yeah, your boy is confused for real! His little secret is that he been boning some chick trying to get his self right, you know. Tryna ungay himself."

Daniel stood up humping the air while in the background we could still hear Chase whimpering from the kitchen.

"You are so fucking wrong for that, Daniel, to just tell his secret like that. He was already going through enough as it was and shit! Asshole!" Megan screamed from the entrance way of the kitchen.

"The truth hurts, don't it muthafucka!" Daniel screams as he grabs another beer and turns it up gulping it down.

"Damn, did I miss something? I mean you taking shit way too personal right now, Danny."

"So what is it? Why the fuck you coming at me like this? Uh," Chase screams, coming out of the kitchen while Megan holds him back. "Why?!"

"Don't act stupid now, bitch, you know why! You went behind my back and tried to holla at my main bitch and tell her about all the shit we had lined up, cock blocking and shit!"

"I ain't telling her nothing!"

"Wait! Ya'll bitches need to settle down and stop this bullshit! Ya'll way too old to be all dramatic and shit! Damn, giving me a fucking headache!"

Tish slams her cup down and paces back and forth.

For about fifteen minutes, no one says anything to each other; we're just eating and getting drunk. Tish started talking.

"Well, since we getting out secrets and all, I became a lesbian right out of high school. My high school sweetheart tried to rape me at prom. My family didn't even believe me, and my dad was never there for me. I think I saw him four times in my life, but I would speak to him on the phone, and all he ever gave me were empty promises.

I remember after high school I was so upset with my family, because my boyfriend at the time was, "Mr. Perfect," and in everyone's eyes he could do no wrong. That summer I left and went to summer school for the college that I got accepted to. I only spent two years there before I dropped out and started again going to school for massage.

I had all of this built up anger in me which led me to drinking and partying all the time, missing class, and my grades suffered, I didn't care. I needed for something to ease the pain that I was feeling, the feeling of being all alone in this world and no one believed me or even cared. They put the blame on me, like I was just trying to ruin his life because he had a full scholarship to play football at a major Ivy League school.

I was the 'temporary girlfriend,' as his mother put it, because when he got to college it would be a whole nother ball game. Then he wouldn't need to waste his time on a high school sweetheart, because there were going to be more qualified girls where he was going. Their families had more money and probably lived in a two-parent home. But little poor Tish had only one parent who worked all the time and no father in her life. I was trash to them.

All of the boys at school were jerks! All they wanted was sex, no love, no getting to know me, love me, they just wanted sex. One night I was sitting on the front stairs of my dorm, drunk as a skunk and completely shit faced. I was approached by this girl and I didn't think anything about it, but she invited me to a party that she was throwing and her and her friend helped me get up and walk down to her dorm. All I know is, when I woke up, it was the next day and she was behind me spooning me. I had no idea how I got there I just remembered stumbling into her dorm room. Then after that, lights out.

would see her around the campus and she never would say anything to me, so one day I just ran her down and started questioning her about that night. I was never in my right mind and whatever happened I was open to it. I mean, I was susceptible to anything that could have happened to me. She said that nothing happened that I didn't want to happen. I got real upset and started choking her and punching her; I was arrested for assault and was kicked out of school actually, so you can say I dropped out, sort of.

Well, after that, I went back home and all of my family thought of me as a failure; I couldn't get it right with the star player, the future millionaire, with life, period! I was worthless and on top of that I now had a drinking problem. I moved out of my parent's house and moved into a homeless shelter, I filled out the application section. Where it had *nearest living relative* I marked 'none.' I was alone and had no family. I had wrote them off as being dead, because they all were dead to me.

I met Shelly when I moved to Atlanta; I jumped on the next thing smoking after spending four months in the homeless shelter. I found out later that my parents had put out a missing person's bulletin on me, but I was grown now and didn't need them anymore. When I got to Atlanta, at the train station, I saw her fighting with her boyfriend. He was being really disrespectful. His rage in his eyes and the way he was manhandling her made me furious! I had to live with my own frustrations, the lies that my ex told on me, and how everyone made me out to be a liar, the long sleepless nights, feeling alone, no family, the alcohol, the depression, no help.

The anger in me made my blood boil, as I concentrated on their argument outside of the train station, out of view of many of the people who were waiting around and who had just exited the train. I ran outside to confront him and to put an end to it all! This was me getting back, for everyone in my life that hurt me and my rage was fuming! I just exploded. He wasn't looking at me when I hit him from the left side of his head, a hard right hook and a knee to the head when he was going down. Once he hit the ground, all hell broke loose. All of my anger surfaced and I kicked him repeatedly in the face, chest, arms and stomach. I lost it!

Shelly stood back with tears running down her face as she watched me beat her boyfriend to a pulp. I just blacked out! When the police pulled me off of him I was covered in blood. He just lay there motionless, making sounds and grunting for a minute, until he started to cough and curled up on his side.

Victory! I had finally got him! In my mind I was giving my ex-boyfriend, my parents, the dean of my college, and anyone who ever took advantage of me, just what they deserved! The expression on Shelly's face was one of horror and relief. I had completely demolished her abusive ex and I came outta nowhere and beat his ass the way he was trying to do to her. The cops read me my rights and hauled me off to jail. 'Welcome to Tish's World, Atlanta' I yelled as they shoved me into the back of the cop car.

On the ride there they interviewed me with like 100 questions, of which I chose to answer all of them with, 'Shut the Fuck Up!' I was arrested again for assault and the charges read, 'Malicious wounding. Assault with a deadly weapon. Assault on an Officer. Obscene gestures and threats.'

What in all the fuck, man! I had no weapons. Well, I guess if you could count these stones and hammers I laid on his ass then that should count for something, Tish mocks as she throws punches and kicks in the air.

My tongue was like a Samurai sword, just cutting, slicing and dicing the ears of those assholes who arrested me. Lucky for me, the person I saved was actually a lawyer who specialized in the same situations that seemed to constantly happen to her. Shelly followed us to the jail and even posted bond for me. When my case came up, she fought for me and all of my charges were dropped. Needless to say, she returned the favor tenfold.

I was looking at some time because of my previous offenses and was ordered to anger management, but I was new to Atlanta and had no place to stay. The little bit of money that I did have had ran out shortly after being free of all of the charges. Shelly asked me to move in with her, as a kind gesture for me saving her life. We hit it off pretty well and became good friends and she helped me get myself back on track and even put in a good word for me when I applied for massage school and I got in. We were roomies and we shared just about everything, just like the family that I never quite had and it felt good.

Shelly had a type, the loud and overbearing assholes who thought that they could just run their women and treat them like shit. For the life of me, I couldn't figure out why she would continue to put up with that shit, especially since I had saved her ass from getting beat by her ex. It was a cycle that had to stop. I would be the one left to comfort and console her after they would either cheat or try to put their hands on her. I had given up the prospect of dating all together and just concentrated on school and being Shelly's damn psychotherapist! It had become so damn draining! And one night I confronted Shelly when she came home late, crying. Jokingly I mentioned, 'It ain't working for you; men are just not your thing. Maybe you need to give women a try. How hard would it be? It don't seem like you are having any luck with them. You might as well.'

I didn't realize it then but I was also telling myself that. I had been so upset with my father, my ex and all the men that I was supposed to be loved by, and at that moment I and Shelly both shared experiences. She looked at me and smiled and we both spoke openly that night and I told her about what happened to me in college and we chose that night to take a step together in that direction. Now, it was all kinds of weird. I had never even thought of touching a woman in that way, or even allowing one to do the same to me. It wasn't a thought; it felt different but good. I released all of my pain and inhibitions. I was free, free to feel something different and new, without the pain and guilt of being a failure to anyone.

She looked at me so different than the world had. I was her savior and everything at that moment, and we expressed that in words and in actions. That night, I had become a lover of myself and that woman. We tasted each other's tears and our hearts connected as our skin touched. I had found someone who knew my pain and would accept and love me for me. And the rest is history!"

Tish jumps up and smacks me across the head.

"Damn! Why the hell you do that?"

"Cause you deserve it, Paulie! Fucking asshole!"

"Well, now that we done gone down memory lane and shit let's talk about business homeboy we still need to talk about it. I wanna know where do we go from here?" Daniel points his finger at Chase as he comes back from the kitchen.

"Fuck you, Daniel! You know I only told you about this shit and you got to go spreading the shit!"

"Fuck you! We are all family here, Chase, and it had to be said. And dude, I'm sorry about all this shit but I just thought you was coming at my girl sideways to fuck my shit up."

"Naw that wasn't even the case. She wanted to know how business was going and was curious to know what we were doing. I ain't even throw you out there like that. If she was going to be a woman about it, she could have just straight up asked was you fucking any other bitches. But instead she ran back to you with another story."

"Damn! Just chill everybody! I know the alcohol is probably making everybody like this, but I just need all of ya'll attention so we can discuss the new business venture I got planned for us.

"First, let's talk about some of the major challenges that we all face, like earning a client's business, keeping the client happy and gaining referrals. Yes, Business 101. And Daniel can exclude the business that you have handled with John; that's a whole different story. I just mean in your personal lives and business, what are the things that we tend to run into that may affect our bottom line? And that's making money and keeping a decent client base."

"I got you, my dude! Well it's kinda hard to say because the very thing that would hurt a massage therapist is actually the thing that I seek outta all of my clients. Now, I hate to say it this way, but… 'Sex.' Daniel starts humping the air again.

"Well damn! How the hell do you even make any money running your business that way, Daniel," Megan questioned him.

"Easy! All my clients are freaks! Yeah, I got a lot of hit or misses here and there, but for the most part, all my clients get down like that, so I don't even have to worry."

"I guess what he is trying to say is that he has selective marketing so as not to get into too much trouble with clients who may not want his services."

"Yeah, just what you said, Paulie! I make sure to ask what they are interested in and if they ain't game I am on to the next one!"

Megan nods her head, "I hear ya but for me it's the other way around. I get tired of guys hitting on me and expecting more out of a massage. I'm like no happy endings no rubbing of penises! Nothing! I have lost quite a few clients because they were looking for more."

"Same here!" Both Tish and Chase blurt out at the same time.

"Believe it or not, plenty of women come on to me and I have to stop them and let them know that it's not that type of party. I am trying to get my money, hunti, and not the cat! Ok?" Chase high fives Tish.

"Now that's the Chase I know, baebae! All about them dollar bills baby," Tish falls back and laughs.

"Yeah, that has to be the most frustrating part of this job is when they want to 'trade' for an hour to two hour massage. Naw, honey, not today! I have busted my ass working on your fucked up body and even doing your feet! You want to 'trade?' Naw, you got the right one. Wrongbitch.com. The domain is for sale, click here to inquire about this domain. Pay me my money and get the hell on!"

"I had the same problem when I first started; it's almost like they don't recognize what we do as a real profession worth them paying money in exchange for service."

"Right! Now I know that it's a very intimate session. You having to trust someone with your body and not to mention those 'spots,' you know what I'm talking about! Don't touch me or kiss me behind the ears. That is my spot!" Tish points to them and shakes.

"Well, thank you for the tip, Tish I will make sure I do that when you are not looking then. BAM! I got you!"

Tish pushes Daniel as they begin to play fight on the couch.

"Those are some good and valid points. The things that are challenges, when we are out there performing our jobs, and I would say hat is the number one issue. And I think communication is key in the beginning, to make sure you don't short yourself with doing a massage and not receiving the money ahead of time. Something I think we all were victims of earlier on in our careers. That 'trade' scenario really hurts the chances of you making money and growing your business, so we have to take a different approach when we're out here as professionals and tighten up our perspective clients."

"So be selective in who we chose?" Megan asked.

"Yes, because if not, then we may end up dealing with the 'trade' type of folks more. I have learned over the years that when you build a rapport and a closed type of sale and order about your work, there is no wiggle room or anything open for them to 'trade' off to devalue your work. For instance, do not give discounts. This is your bread and butter and be firm on your pricing. When you give discounts or even change your price in mid-pitch to earn a customer, then that devalues your worth. Remember, you have spent countless hours in school and have earned the equivalent of what doctors have to learn, not to mention the cost, and you know what you are doing. Stop giving discounts! So what if you lose that customer, stick to your guns."

"You hit that one right on the head! You are so right! I noticed that when I don't keep a business mind and really watch the clients that I choose, I run into it a lot," Megan shakes her head.

"So you saying to profile your perspective clients? That's not fair, my dude?"

"No, what's not fair is that you waste your time and gas money to go to a client's house. Then they don't want to pay you for your time and they were already planning not to pay you. So don't cheat yourself. It's not profiling, it's just knowing your client and knowing if it's going to even be worth your time and money to entertain that person.

Those are the hard facts. It's better to try and eliminate or reduce that from happening, which brings me to my next solution. Deposits! Make sure you get a deposit before you go, I don't care if its $10, make sure that at least they are serious about it and it secures them a time and place. This is a sure fire way to reduce that issue, not getting rid of that issue all together, but at least you have something paid towards your time. This weeds out the 'trade' type of folks because they normally want things done for free."

"That is a great idea, Paulie! I see now why my business was suffering. I needed to conduct my business just like this."

"That's true, Megan, and it works and has been working for me ever since I started and earned these contracts. We are not here to do anyone a favor; we will give them a service, a paid service. That is the only trade I am interested in. What we do is very personal and intimate, so we have to set boundaries with our customers so that they know we are not violating them; in turn, we do not want to be violated. When we build a rapport with them, we have earned their trust, which should never be broken if you want to keep them as a client.

I used to think that all I had to do was just find a client, do the massage and send them on their way after they paid me. That was the furthest thing from the truth. You have to invest some of yourself with them, you have to become one of my hardest terms to come to grips with, a 'friend.' We have to be friend-like, friendly with our clients, having great customer service. They have to feel like they matter and not just a number, you understand. That is the key to keeping them happy and ultimately helping them stay as a customer and even give you referrals."

"Here's one that you never covered, my dude. Having sex with a client and then it becomes more than that, she wants to be in a relationship with you!"

"That's why you separate business and pleasure. Always stay professional, if you can. I messed up and went against my own set of rules, having sex with one of my clients, and I don't expect to ever be with that client romantically or even in a relationship, because it just won't work."

"Good word and info, my dude! Yeah, cause you will never hear the end of it if you do. What you doing? You going to give a massage? Are you gonna give her the same massage you gave me? Remember? You fucked me, right? My dude, you will never have another client again as long as you are with her; I bet you that! But please, enough of this shit. What's going on with the new business venture you talking about?"

"Yes, it is a fine line indeed when mixing business and pleasure unless..."

Daniel interrupts me.

"It's all pleasure, baby!"

"True!" Megan yells out, as she looks up from my book.

"I will be sending you all a packet to fill out on Monday, so send them to me as soon as you are done with them, so we can get everything processed quickly. I want to jump on it right away since they are saying there is more than one company interested in this contract."

Everyone nods their heads and we all enjoy the rest of the night .Chase and Tish had both settled down and were back at it being their own selves. Megan goes back to reading my book and I could see that she was deep into it, so much so that she couldn't even hear Tish calling her name.

"Megan! Megan! Damn, girl! That shit must be good. You can't hear a word I'm saying, lol!"

"Uh, yeah, it's real good, girl."

We continued our conversations, catching up with one another, with work, life and everything else in-between. By the end of the night everyone was drunk and tired. I called a car to come take everyone home and assured them their cars would be safe at my house. They could just call me when they were ready to come pick them up.

Tish reminded me, "Paulie, don't forget you still owe us a dinner date."

She whispered in my ear as she walked out the front door.

Deep Tissue

"It's War! My hands declare war on your body. Hand to hand skin to skin...in this battle we are both winners."

This was her first professional massage and my first day on the job. I had done over 950 hours of massage during my training in school, but this would be the 1-hour that it would count the most. I greeted her and instructed her on filling out the intake form and to answer the questions to her best ability. She seemed nervous and I was a little, also. She finished the intake form and I retrieved it from her and sat down in the receiving room to go over it. She mentioned that she was ticklish just about everywhere but her butt. I ran over her file with her and pulled my supervisor over to the side, once she was all settled on the table.

"Now I know we are not supposed to speak about anyone's chart, but this one seemed kinda strange. She's ticklish everywhere but her butt."

The supervisor told me, "If that's what she prefers then you will have to do it; she is a paying customer."

He hands me back the form with a hard jab to the chest and a smile. In my mind I kept telling myself, *Stay professional and just follow the customer's request.*

Once in the room, I closed the door behind me, putting the chart in the pocket near the door. She was up under the covers, all covered up from head to toe, the foot booster was laying on the floor next to the chair where her clothes were thrown; skirt, shirt and bra falling off the chair.

She whispered, Are we alone?"

"Yes," I answered.

She then threw the covers back revealing her nude body as she laid face down.

"I'm so tense," she moaned. "I only want you to massage my butt."

There she laid, totally nude, as I marveled at her beauty.

Her body, laying there near the candlelight. As the flames flicker, my eyes follow in and out of shadows as every inch of her is revealed to me.

Following her curves from her round breast that lay on the table as she looked up at me, waiting for me to service her. I could see the curve of her spine that led to two of the most shapely mounds I have ever seen. She saw where my eyes were looking and she raised her hips in the air so that I could get a better view. Gently shaking her hips from side to side and taking one hand to massage her full breast, she looked at me with a devilish grin.

I snapped out of it, I had a job to perform and not get caught up in whatever she was trying to do to tempt me. This was my first day on the job; I didn't want it to be my last. I prepared the oil and rubbed until it was warm in my hands. Firmly placing my hands on her rear end I started the massage.

It was apparent that my hands were getting out more than just tension. With every stroke came a new sound. I started doing circles with my hands, grasping and cupping her waist, hips and buttocks. Her body started to mimic my hand movements.

"Harder!" she moaned, while her hips rocked back and forth.

I placed my hands around the small of her back, gliding around with even deeper strokes, cupping her gluts and spreading them as I went. She arched her back, revealing her shapely rear in full view of her wet pulsating vaginal lips. As I massaged, her moans began to go higher and higher. I could no longer hide my interest, as my penis pressed against my scrubs. My bulge and scent of precum latent boxers must've fully awakened her senses. She reached out and grabbed my rock hard penis, recovering it from my pants. She stroked it as a wave of passion came over me. She had expressed her true intentions for this massage session and I was willing to reciprocate.

Running my tongue down the nape of her neck, lapping at her earlobe, lips closing on the top of her ear, swirling around her inner ear, she arched her back and moaned. I took long deep breaths as I passionately engulfed her whole ear, releasing it with short blows over the wetness left behind. As I glided down to the base of her ass she shook in anticipation and it gave her goose bumps. In turn, I give her soft kisses on every one of them. Spreading her legs apart, facing downward, my tongue rolled over her, stopping and circling her anus, darting, licking and pleasuring her as she squirmed. As she reached another climax, I stuffed the pillowcase in her mouth and forced her head back to the massage table. Catching every drop, I spread her lips and savored her juices trailing down onto my waiting tongue.

She turned around. I inserted two fingers in her; she bent over and swallowed the head of my penis with a moan, tasting the precum with her cool wet tongue. My nature rose as she stroked my rock hard shaft and sucked the remainder, hitting the back of her throat.

Pushing her back down on to her back I descend on her, feverishly sucking and licking her clit with steady deliberate strokes on the top and left sides of her pearl. I sensed her orgasm was near. I flattened my tongue and sucked harder with her legs pressed up in the air. Bucking wildly, she squirted hot juices into my awaiting mouth once again. My fingers stroked her until she laid motionless, pulsating and moaning...

I didn't want to show him that I was a bit interested in him, but my nipples would not let me hide my interest. Poking out of my tank top at attention I caught him taking a peak as our eyes met.

"How do you want me," he asked as he mounted the table, fully undressed holding a towel over his stomach and private area.

I motioned to him to lay on his stomach with his head into the face cradle. I had to calm my nerves because the site of him excited me. My nipples strained to stay tame through the cotton tank top and when he let out a deep breath along with a low whistling sound, the moment my hands touched his skin, I could feel an instantaneous explosion between my legs. That tingling sensation traveled from my ears curving my lips to a smile that I quickly tamed immediately with my teeth, biting my bottom lip. The feeling was not lost in my lip biting, it was too late and now it had traveled down my spine both anterior and posterior. I tensed up, trying to fight it as the small of my back flexed, pulling my glutes together. Trying hard to hold on to this eruption that pained me so much that I too let out a gasp of air, trying my best to hide what had just happened.

Too late; he had noticed it also, prompting him to ask, "Are you ok?"

I couldn't answer. I just shook my head running my hands over his body, smooth muscles, and skin so soft, he took another deep breath as I finished the stroke. I had to take a pause because the sexual tension was a bit too much. I walked around the table; at the time I started walking he started to stretch his arms outward. They grazed my thighs and ended up between my legs. I stopped and pressed my legs together; his hand and arm was in a vise grip and I wasn't planning on letting go. This got his attention as his hand moved up my thighs and found my soaking wet pussy waiting for his touch. He circled my clit with his fingers. As he penetrated me, I fell to my knees.

As he got up from the table I noticed that he was fully erect. The head of his penis danced as the veins that surrounded it were full. He placed his hand over his shaft, massaging it and stroking it as he grabbed my head and led me to it. Opening my mouth wide, he inserted it into my mouth. I tasted his precum, salty and slippery as it danced on my tongue and I swallowed every bit of it.

By now my inner thighs were throbbing and my nipples were extra sensitive to the touch. Without a word he came down to the floor right beside me and grabbed my breasts, placing one in his mouth and firmly squeezing the other. I pushed him off me and motioned for him to get back on the table; he did as I directed.

He laid on his back as I mounted him, grabbing a hold of his penis head. I was both excited and nervous; it was bigger than any I had ever had before. He grabbed my waist in a hurry to drag me down onto him, so I pushed out my arms and slowed him down. I gently eased my way onto him. I could feel the pressure as it parted my lips and the tingling sensation again took over my body, sending pulses through my spine and into my nipples and made them push out even more, The steady motion of his hips pushing his penis further in and me using my legs to reduce how far he was gonna go, I kept it up for about five minutes until I was nice and wet to fully take it all. As I opened up, the gentle back and forth not only put pressure on the inside of my walls but also pulled on my labia where my clit was exposed and rubbed against his shaft every time he pulled out and went back in. This sent a sensation that made me feel like going to the bathroom. I tried to control the motion but he took over, pushing deep inside of me; the pressure and pain almost knocked me out.

Deep thrusts into me, I could feel every inch of him touching areas in me I hadn't even discovered. The feeling was so new I held back the tears. Our bodies rolled in a rhythmic dance with spots of pleasurable pain, almost capsizing, falling into a deep void, as all of it built up and warmed to a great explosion. I found myself in Nirvana, my feelings connected to a deep abyss of nothingness, immeasurable bliss savoring the moment of extraction. Our bodies drenched in sweat, I felt him inside of me erupting and I jumped off as he emptied his load, aiding him as I stroked his penis until my hand was covered...

I cleaned up the mess he made, wondering to myself, *How can something so damn big make such an uncontrollable mess?* It didn't surprise me a bit though; it's to be expected. Big men can be messy at times. He pointed to his neck and motioned for me to follow him to the table. He laid down on the table, pulling his shirt off as the crumbs fell all over my rug. This brute needed to learn some house manner. I stopped in my tracks just peering over his very muscular body, his deep cleft when his lower back met his round glutes and monstrous legs, made my heart skip a beat. His rear end was so shapely it poked up in the air as he laid down on his stomach. What a beautiful site.

Wow, I said to myself as I stroked and called out the name of each muscle: Traps, Rhomboid major minor, Levator Scapulae, Serratus Anterior, Latissimus dorsi, External Obliques, QL's, Iliac crest, Sacrum, Gluteus Maximus....

Lost in a trance of naming muscles, I was hypnotized. As my hands battled with digging deep into the crevices of his muscles, he let out deep moans and reacted to each stroke, moving his body from side to side. Every now and then I had to tap him to keep him from moving.

It was nearly impossible to perform my massage with this man moving so much that he almost fell of my table more than once. I figured that he must have been ticklish because each time I stroked near his hips he would squirm like a little kid being tickled. He started to arch his back and move his hips around, almost like an invitation to tell me to move my hands further down. I caught on to his movements and understood just what he wanted. Reaching between his legs I grasped the family jewels, cuffing it with one hand and using my fingers to soothe the urogential diaphragm, sup-transverse perineal area circling the perineal ody. This really got a reaction out of him, not the one that you would expect, like jumping up with excitement to question me what I was doing. It was mutual; he knew his circular motions of his hips asked me to dive right on in. Having my hands on his pulse, feeling each time the inrush of blood came in filling up his already swollen nut sack, reaching under and grabbing a hold of his shaft, made him release a sigh followed by a deep grunt. He was fully erect and ready to reciprocate my total assault on him, but I definitely had a surprise for him alright.

See I couldn't believe that he would actually pay for a massage from me and I don't know why I would even accept taking him as a client, being that we had history and bad blood. This prick had assaulted me, embarrassed me and damaged my character, along with having me lose a lot of my clients. Payback was an understatement now. It was evident that he was swinging both ways, from his attempts to tease me and that kiss. He was no stranger to this side of the fence but he was not going to get my cookie. I had him right where I needed him, I pulled my bag closer to the table and assured him to just calm down as he was trying to get up and turn over. I stroked him some more as he relaxed. With both hands on his ass I pushed his glute muscles apart and he aided me with spreading his legs apart, I assumed for me to gain better access to him. I inspected his anus and it was tight, not damaged from backdoor entry at all; it looked like he never had been penetrated in that way before.

He tried again to move off the table, I pushed him down with some force and licked his nut sack; he settled down real quick. Reaching into my bag, I grabbed the syringe that a friend of mine had supplied to me, with a cocktail of goody juice already filled to the tip. One quick poke and that's all it took. He squirmed for a little bit but then stopped. I asked him if he was ok and he answered back that he was fine and wanted to know what that was. He asked if he was bitten by something, but I assured him it was a mosquito. He laid back down and asked me to continue.

The rage and hurt that I felt from the times that he embarrassed and assaulted me played in my head at that moment, so fresh that I knew what I was about to do was going to be payback enough. He tried his best to fight it but his arms were like limp noodles; he could not fight back at all. I took my time to prepare my assault. Walking around the table I stripped in front of him, and he looked at me, dazed and drugged, with his tongue hanging out of his mouth, just in the right place, I thought to myself, but first I gave him a show so he could see what he would never have. Turning on my stereo I slid a mixed CD in that I made the night before. I got into position and twerked right in front of him, bucking, swaying my hips, dropping it down to the floor, earth quaking it and spreading my cheeks so that he could get a good look at what he would never taste or feel. Looking him in his eyes, I could tell that he was excited and trying his best to move off the table. I approached the table and moved my crotch right in front of his face. He tried to lick me with his tongue but I pulled back; his eyes followed me as I kept teasing him.

I pushed him off of the table and his body hit the floor like a sack of potatoes. He groaned and rolled around to his back. Lifting his legs up, pulling him close to me now, I mounted him, rubbing our skin together looking him in his eyes. He smiled in anticipation of what was coming next.

Sliding back, I grabbed his penis and raised his nut sack, inserting my fully erect green condom fitted 10 incher! His eyes damn near popped out of his head as I struggled to push past his tight virgin asshole. He grunted and stared at me in agony as I stroked him in pure ecstasy. I was able to get all of me deep inside of him stroking him from the tip to the base of my shaft. The pressure surrounding my penis made my blood flow into it even more as the sounds of his grunts turned into pleasurable moans, he relaxed as his limp penis became erect again. I stroke him as I buried my penis deep inside of him; the sweat from his thighs ran down my chest hairs and dripped back down into the crack of his ass, lubricated his anus and making it easier for me to glide deeper in him.

He closed his eyes and held on to my arm that was holding his enormous thigh up as I switched positions laying him on his side. I could feel him shaking and his legs tensed up as I felt this. I felt a rumble inside my nut sack. The in and out and sensation at the end of my stroke massaging the tip of my head, I was about to cum and my stroke began to harden. I reached over to help him with his climax, but too late. He had erupted, shooting cum all over my hand as I reached over and I dropped over his hip as I climaxed filling my condom. I was shaking and emptied of my load as he reached back and brought me in closer to him, urging me to cuddle him. Tears rolled down his eyes as I pulled out of him. He reached back, grabbing my dick, stroking it. Pushing him off of me I jumped up.

"Now how do you feel," I yelled at him. "Now you my little bitch!"

I like to feel I can control myself and often people have a hard time with knowing how deep my heart really loves. I love to give pleasure but it's hard to receive the pleasure in return. I am very particular in who I share my body with and I know that not all are created equal. I have found that in order for me to have a good orgasm I must be relaxed, desired, mentally seduced, stimulated, and physically warmed up by an affectionate touch. Once all of those things occur, I start to feel a pressure building in my clit, and the middle of me starts to get creamy. Then it starts to run down my ass and thigh. If I have to wait for it, then sliding fingers into me and rubbing my clit will help do the trick. I must feel safe sexually to jump off that cliff. I find it difficult for me to cum at times; you have to be able to look into my eyes to see that I'm not as reserved as they may perceive me to be...

This is my escape, you know how to touch me and to connect to my inner feelings without saying a word; yes, the eyes have it all. I love the smell of you, the sweet scents and over-powering taste of your luscious treat that I savor and it follows me the whole day… the sights and the sounds which get me excited, to hear your breath. Feeling the warmth of your breath on my neck, the sensation sends me into a daydream. On the brink of losing control, taking me to a place where I normally could hold back and release a little bit of pleasure, but that's not possible.

I feel my body getting warmer and warmer, my breasts start swelling at your touch and rubbing and sucking of my nipples with the perfect pressure. I find myself letting go and not caring how wild an explosion of exquisite pleasure of wetness, moaning, sweating and trembling of an orgasm. He matches that feeling; I can't even lie. And if you have not been blessed to have him, I am not stingy, I am willing to share.

Pushing his pulsating dick inside of me at the perfect spot, while I'm clenching onto my bottom lip and his back, savoring that divine moment of extreme body movement. I think to myself...*Ohh did he make me do that?* And I have to answer, *Yes he did, taking me to a place where I had never been fully.*

You know you get close to that feeling but never quite get there. I want you but I know that the timing is all wrong; maybe in another lifetime we would have worked out. I don't like stepping on anyone's toes. To me, I see you as perfect and it just reminds me of warm breezes flowing through our hands as our fingertips interlock, between our palms where once a bit of warm air resided, how our heartbeats meet and love vibes collide, a gentle nudge from you as the excitement fills inside of you at each pop. The bang and explosion of gun powder filled rockets racing to the heavens, I squeeze your hand tighter as your silhouette catches my eye. I gaze on you as I take in the majestic show in the sky and see your shine, hues of blues, greens and purples, colors of love, come closer to me, my love. Such a beautiful sight, not complete, only if the almost perfect was you with me tonight. Baby, you know that I am game; I just want to be with you and not complicate this situation anymore. Ok then it's settled.

We couldn't get our clothes off fast enough, kissing and grabbing on each other while trying to take each item of clothing off. Finally, clothes thrown on the floor, couch and ceiling fan, litter the house, I sit back, taking in the beauty. Jet black hair that falls down below her shoulders, full of curls, each and every piece placed perfectly; even when it's messy she looks like an angel. Her almond shaped eyes seems to pierce my soul, begging me to comfort her, touch her, hug her, because I am familiar with the hurt that lies so deep inside. I follow every angle of her body as she slowly takes off her thong; as she bends over, the rays from the dawn light her shape, full legs and hips... cherry red thong fashioned with lace hits the floor and she returns to a standing position, reaching behind to undo her bra. Her breasts, full golden brown with dark chocolate areolas that surround nipples the size of dimes, perky and sticking out as they descend and bounce from the release of the bra. She motions for me to come closer to her, reaching out to me. As we embrace, pushing her soft breasts against my chest, I hold her tight kissing her deeply. We wrestle with each other's lips interlocking, tongues trading sweet saliva; I get a handful of hair and pull her head to the side, diving into her neck with slight nibbles, kisses and licks. Finding her sweet spot right below her right ear I work my way up to the bottom of her earlobe, circling with my tongue and grabbing on lightly to it, sucking and flicking on it as it drove her wild. I could fell her legs buckle as I blew a warm stream over her neck and ear. The reaction caused her to grab on to me and bring me closer, as she dropped one arm from around my neck, searching my body downward until she reached the head of my penis, which was rubbing against her inner thigh. She massaged it and wiped the precum over the head. Pulling her hand away, she brings it to her mouth; she opened up wide and drenched it with her tongue returning it back to the head of my penis. Stroking it as we both groped each other's bodies feverishly.

Tripping over clothes we found ourselves in the middle of my living room, me trying to catch her as she fell towards the couch. She falls upright while my face fell forward into her lap. Without missing a beat I aimed for her inner thighs, kissing, sucking and groping again. As my hand runs the full length of her legs, stopping only to put pressure on an erect left leg, kissing and sucking behind the knee, this drove her crazy. As she squirmed and kicked, I held on tighter, closing my eyes as I concentrated on the erogenous zone, which set her on fire. She could no longer take the pleasure that I was delivering and she kicked me, knocking me to the floor, where she straddled my face. She directed me to "stay;" I complied. She sat her hips right above my face and moved her hips within inches of my touch, stopped me from getting a taste of her sweet flower and just waving it above me. I was more than excited; I had remembered her sweet smell and taste and was in great anticipation to have more. She teased me, rubbing herself and I could feel the drops hit my face as she worked herself over me, I reached up to grab her hips to bring her down to chin level but she resisted and kept playing with herself.

I couldn't take anymore. I was rock hard and wanted to sink my tongue into her, have her squirt on my face as she had done before. Her screams and moans were so addictive I needed and wanted to hear them once more. I reached up and cupped both breasts in my hands, circling the nipples with wet fingers. She bucked wildly; being very sensitive in her breasts made her juices flow even more. I could hear from the manipulation from her fingers she was on the verge of letting go a heavy orgasm. Noisy and wet I enjoyed the show that I was restricted in taking part in. I massaged her ass as I opened and closed her cheeks, using my left hand to reach back towards her anus, lightly circling it and forcing her hips down towards my face with my right hand. She still held on; even through the double stimulation she was poised until it became too much. She exploded with a loud scream, dropping the weight of her body on my chest and chin and what followed was a myriad of juices; she bucked wildly as she squirted all over my face.

Now my tongue laid deep inside her, probing, licking and circling her clit. I stroked it and sucked it as she danced on my chest. She was on the verge of erupting again, then she forced both hands over my face. I closed my eyes as I could feel the motion of her body, rocking back and forward as I enjoyed a mouthful of her juices. She trembled from time to time and I could feel her tensing up each time she was about to climax again.

She removed her hand off my face, apologizing and asking if she had hurt me. I was perfectly ok. She was just so into it, and the feeling took over her whole body, she remarked and I understood quite well. My penis was throbbing and standing at attention, hard and ready to explode. She reached behind her and stroked it a few times while I pulled her closer to my lips, sucking and fingering her. Without asking me, she pulled out a silk scarf and began to wrap it around my eyes. I could feel her turning around. She grabbed my penis and inserted it into her mouth.

Feeling her cool, wet tongue and her soft hands around my shaft made me stiffen up. I reached out and could feel her round hips and legs, grabbing them and pulling them closer to my body. Spreading her legs and pushing back towards me, her wet vaginal lips and mine met. I gave them a long deep tongue kissing. I savored her juices and my ears felt warm with delight hearing her hum quietly over my penis as it went in and out of her mouth. She finished each stroke with a long lick from her dripping mouth.

Licking her inner thighs and base of her vaginal opening, I inserted two fingers. She sat up and I could feel her weight pressing down on my chin. I licked and probed more. I felt her cool hand stroking my dick as she massage my sack with her other hand. I ran my tongue up and down her lips and ended with a long stroke over her anus, which made her jump. Holding on to her hips, I let my tongue go in a more direct motion, trained on the opening of her anus. She teased me a little, moving away from me, then she allowed me to pull her in, grasping her hips and guiding her back down. I flicked my tongue over and over again until she pushed her total weight onto my face. My tongue entered her and she shook uncontrollably. I felt a stream of juices run down my chin and puddle right around my neck and chest. She laid down over my body still shaking as the she stroked my penis.

She turned her body around and I could feel the little prickle of newly shaven hairs touch my upper lips through the wetness that drenched her inner thighs. Her clit protruded and I reached out with my tongue and lips as she moved closer to me, grinding her hips on my chin. At that moment I could feel her grabbing my penis again and the tip of it was surrounded by wetness, this time it was not her hand. Descending down on me and I could feel the pulsating vagina walls of a mystery woman.

My mind raced; I tried to reach for the blindfold but my arms were met with two pairs of soft hands. I relaxed and I could feel her grinding on me and before long she was bouncing up and down on my hard shaft. The weight of her thighs and the smack each time our laps met forced my sensation of climaxing in my mind to within five minutes of her mounting me. I struggled not to cum because my mind was fixed on finding out just who this mystery woman was, but after a while I didn't care. They took turns, one on my face and the other riding me. Her taste and smell was just as tantalizing as my muse, and the one distinction I could make was that her vaginal lips were fuller; when she sat on my face it was like a full on suction cup that never stop pulling at my lips. They guided me up, still blindfolded, as I grasped a pair of hips, inserting my penis into her and slow stroking her. I could feel just where she would react each time I slid in and I made sure that I intentionally stroked that same spot until she exploded all over me. The feeling of her skin bouncing back to me and the sounds, the moaning, sent me over the edge. The one last stroke pushed back hard on my shaft, as all of my cum bubbled up in my sack and pushed through my penis. I pulled out with streams of it spraying over her butt.

I heard her finally yell out as she had moaned the whole while. "Yes baby I'm cumming!"

Pulling the blind fold off I knew I heard a familiar voice.

"Tish?" I asked in disbelief.

DEEP TISSUE

CONFESSIONS OF A MASSAGE THERAPIST THE REVEAL

What will be the outcome of Paul's threesome with Tish and Shelly? How will they progress from this point on? Find out all of your questions along with catching up with the other friends and see what's in store for everyone and their new business venture.

Here's a Sneak Peak –The Reveal:

"Tish?!" I asked again taking the silk scarf off of my eyes.

"Yes Paulie, it's me. Hell I didn't want to miss all of the fun. Anyway Shelly told me, and she thought that it would be a good idea. Well now I see just what she was head over hills for...Damn baby you don't have to stop."

I looked over at Shelly who looked back at me as if to say to keep on going. She winked her eye at me without saying a word she grabbed Tish's head and buried it into her crouch. Shelly's head dropped back against the headboard and she began to moan. Tish grabbed a hold of my penis and guided it back towards her. Shelly's moans really got to me, it awoken a beast inside of me that made me want to just dive right back into what we had been doing five minutes earlier. I zoned out, thinking about the first time I had sex with Shelly, the touch the feeling the smells and sounds. I could not at the moment ignore the softest and juiciest feeling that I was currently feeling from Tish.

Tish's body is a gift; she normally would wear baggy clothes, hiding her figure. She had more curves than Shelly, full and firm breast with round and long nipples, her mid section was well toned, her hips and thighs were round and thick her butt was voluptuous and round. I couldn't keep my hands off of caressing her from hips to thighs to lower back. Her vaginal walls squeezed my penis and contracted with a rhythmic pulse, she had very good control of which made me climax fast. We were far from being done.

Tish mounted me; her soft thighs touching my legs, descending down onto my shaft and landing, I could feel every inch of her orgasmic flower and I reached out to welcome her on top of me. We embraced and locked into a passionate kiss.

'Damn' I thought to myself. She felt so damn good. Shelly who? I thought. I wanted more of Tish as we became lost in each other. I noticed that Shelly stood back and watched playing with herself as Tish climaxed time and time again and we exchanged sessions of tongue kissing and fondling each others chest and thigh areas. Tish shook and applied more pressure at her hips to mine as her eyes rolled in the back of her head. Shelly embraced her while sitting directly on my face exposing her wet flower right over me, I reached out and grabbed her hips bringing her right down to my face as I dove into her. Her moans and movements excited me even more. I could hear her and Tish lapping kissing and moaning. As Shelly erupted I could feel her buck and shake and then her love drenched my face at the same time I could feel a flow of warm liquids splash on my stomach and drip down towards my shaft bottom wetting my nut sack. From that I exploded holding onto Shelly's legs devouring her, stiffening up, I felt Tish jump up removing the condom and taking my seed deep down her throat, followed by Shelly, she dismounted me and I watched as they both took enjoyment of swallowing my seed and massaging my shaft.

We all laid there for a while looking into space. My mind journeyed back to how it all started. I dozed off. Waking up I found both Tish and Shelly were gone out of the bedroom. I could hear music playing downstairs and smell breakfast being made. I got up and went to the bathroom to take a shower and get my mind together. I could not believe what just happened. Tish was so upset with me the last time that we were around each other; Shelly assured me that she wanted to just be with me and now this!? Man this was crazy, I kept wiping my eyes in the shower because this all had to be a dream. I heard the ladies downstairs going back and forth almost sounded like they were arguing until I heard Tish laughing out loud.

"Girl! I can't believe how good he is! Damn! I ain't even mad at ya! Now I understand how you feel and think about him!"

"Yes! I didn't want to be the one to say 'I told you so' but...I told you so!" Shelly yells loudly as they both breakout in laughter.

Well damn, that's how they think of me as a piece of meat. Lol ohh well I guess now I'm in a love triangle. Just thinking about the conversation that I and Shelly had the other day and how she wanted just me and her, now things are going to be different I see.

DEEP TISSUE

CONFESSIONS OF A MASSAGE THERAPIST

The Reveal

"Q"

Follow the Anthology of Simms Books Publishing...

THE DEVIL'S ANGEL

7 PRACTICAL STEPS FOR EXECUTIVE ASCENSION
THE AFRICAN AMERICAN VOID AND HOW YOU CAN FILL IT

HUMANE INTENTIONS
VOL. 1

MY TRIALS AND ERRORS
REFLECTIONS OF A SINGLE FATHER

SIMMS BOOKS

The Murry Rose

ANGELA MARCUS
SECRETS IN Loom

A Taste of Honey

JACOB 'JC' WRIGHT
11/4/1987 - 01/13/2009
Never Forgotten

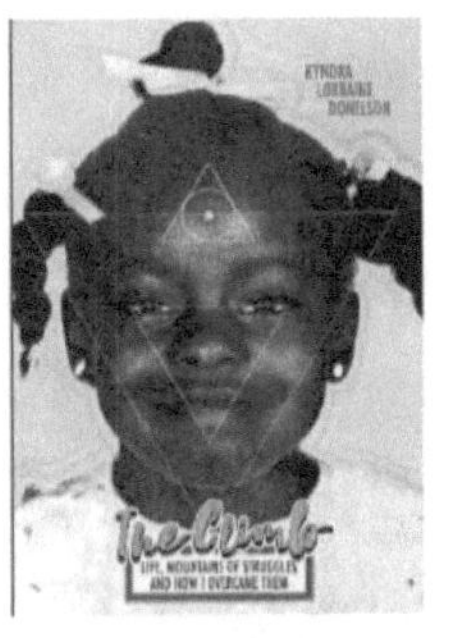

DEEP TISSUE
CONFESSIONS OF A MASSAGE THERAPIST

Morning
Coffee
James R. Simms

Within
His
Skin
CLARITY
SIMMS BOOKS PUBLISHING

SIMMS
BOOKS

ARISING
OF A
LEGENDARY SON
KINGDAWUD MUJAHID BURGESS

The Murry Rose
THE FORBIDDEN ROSE
THE MURRY ROSE SAGA
C. H. FORTENBERRY

7 PRACTICAL STEPS
FOR
EXECUTIVE ASCENSION
THE AFRICAN AMERICAN VOID
AND HOW YOU CAN FILL IT
JONATHAN ROBERTS, PH.D

The Murry Rose
BATTLE FOR THE ROSE
THE MURRY ROSE SAGA
C. H. FORTENBERRY

This is only the beginning...

www.ingramcontent.com/pod-product-compliance
Lightning Source LLC
Chambersburg PA
CBHW021019120726
47905CB00009B/3092